GALLERY NIGHTS

THE BARDO TRILOGY - 2

MALA NAIDOO

Publisher: Independent

www.malanaidoo.com

First Published in Australia 2020

Naidoo, Mala

Title: *Gallery Nights*

ISBN — 978-0-6484854-9-0 (Print)

— 978-0-6488090-0-5 (eBook)

ABOUT THE AUTHOR

Mala Naidoo is an Australian author. She was born in South Africa during the apartheid era which is the impetus for her fictional stories that take on a life of their own when the creative muse beckons. Mala's novels and short-stories empower the voiceless in upholding that literature speaks through the values and culture, angst and joy, of characters' life situations and choices to create connections to a moment in time, an event or conversation, highlighting the universality of our existence.

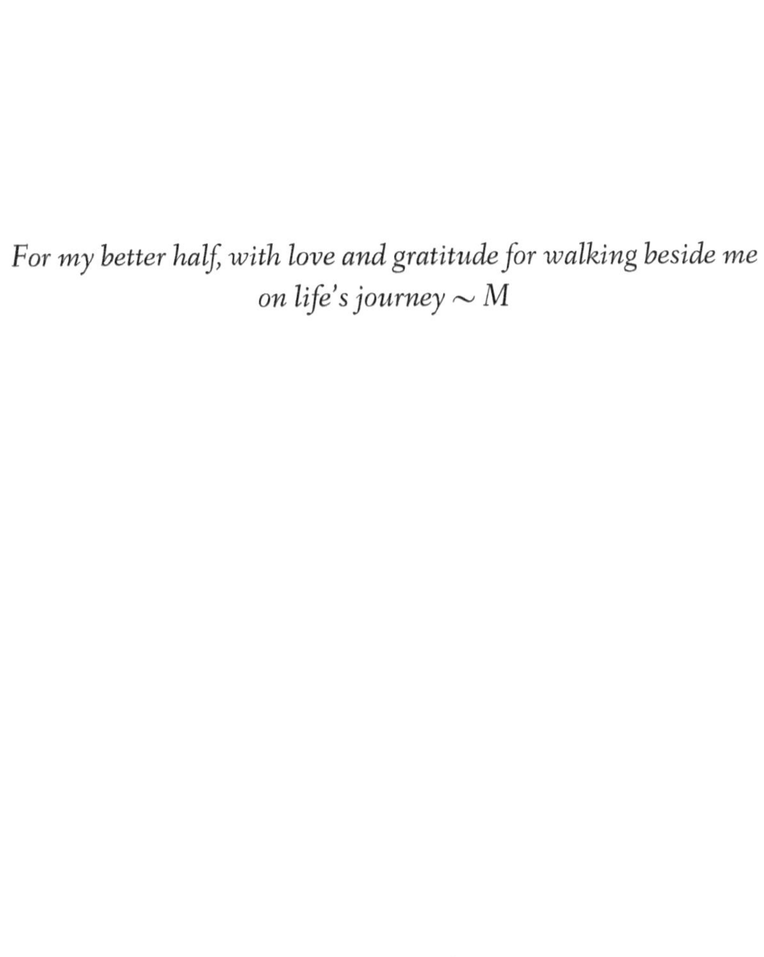
For my better half, with love and gratitude for walking beside me
on life's journey ∼ M

I am all the daughters of my father's house...
Twelfth Night - William Shakespeare

Her father was not at the airport to meet her.

After many months of persuading Viola to come to him for Christmas, he was not there to hug her, to call out in his characteristic warm caramel tones, *Artista, darling you are here!*

Part of her was annoyed but niggling fear surfaced. It was not like him not to deliver on his promise without an explanation. He was her lighthouse and her anchor, her father for all seasons.

She scanned throngs of eager faces, waiting, searching, eyes glued to the passenger exit door, expecting to see loved ones emerge. Viola strolled into the dense crowd, a uniform-clad police officer walked towards her. Her mind raced with uneasy thoughts of what had happened to her father.

The grave look on the officer's face was enough to tell her that something dreadful had happened.

'Ms Viola Bardo?'

A small voice in her head denied her name.

'Why are you here? Where is my father?'

The child returned when anxiety gripped the often controlled, calm Viola.

'Please come with me, Ms Bardo.'

He reached out to guide her through the crowd. She ignored his extended hand.

'Ms Bardo, it is imperative that you comply for the safety of your father.'

This was not what she expected. He implied something had happened to her father. How could it be? She spoke to him yesterday afternoon. He was in good spirits and had plans for what they would do while she was in Porto. Questions pummeled her brain, but her heart was too heavy to heave the words into her mouth. She followed the police officer, head lowered, clutching her bags, unsure of what awaited her.

'Is my father ill? Has he been in an accident? I spoke to him yesterday afternoon. He can't be ill, right?'

'Ms Bardo, I can't say anything just yet, but trust me you will know what you need to know soon enough.'

Tears fogged her vision, and her nose dripped in her fight to control her welling emotions. What cruel fate was this? This had to be a dream. She needed reassurance.

'Please all I ask is to know if my papa is safe?'

'He is, I cannot say any more than that, please, madam.'

Viola's call to her father rang out — no response from him was unusual.

'Where are you taking me?'

'We are on the way to your father's art gallery.'

She sighed, relaxed her intertwined fingers and sat back in the seat.

Her father was running an artist-in-residence program. It was in its final week, she deduced, from their conversations while she was in Athens. She contemplated whether there had been a robbery overnight at the gallery, and perhaps because of a police investigation, her father could not meet her at the airport.

'Is my father in any trouble?'

'I don't have an answer to that question, Ms Bardo. Please no further questions until you talk to your father.'

This shred of reassurance, that she could speak to her father, was enough for now.

The drive from the airport to the gallery took longer than the usual forty minutes. As the police vehicle hit the dirt track from the entrance to the narrow driveway, the magnified, crunching grind of tires on gravel hurt her ears. At the end of the long, winding driveway the gallery appeared — majestic and silent — her father's pride and joy.

He moved to Portugal after her aunt's disappearance, retreating into his artistic world to the exclusion of all social interactions except for her yearly visits.

The grass and trees along the driveway were in prime condition. Her father spent all his life savings on the purchase and renovation of this sprawling property that housed ten self-contained units for visiting artists. He stopped renting out the cottages in recent years preferring his solitude in this tranquil environment. But with age, arthritis slowed Placido Bardo's noted high volume of work. The artist-in-residence revamp was Viola's suggestion to rebuild his finances to maintain his once popular gallery.

A police officer stood at the entrance. Her throat tightened, and her belly churned, petrified by what she was about to hear. Her heart skipped a beat when her father stepped onto the veranda at the main doorway. He was dressed in a crumpled white cotton shirt and linen pants. His ruffled hair revealed distress and exhaustion. Viola jumped out the car before the vehicle came to a complete halt.

'Papa! Papa! I was so worried!'

'Ah, Artista, I knew you would be. I am unharmed so don't worry, please.'

He guided her into the gallery and hugged her like he would never let her go.

'Would you like some coffee or espumante?'

'Nothing, papa, nothing thank you.'

'Really? How about some sparkling water?'

'That will be good, thank you.'

The prominent portrait of her aunt Lorenza with her Mona Lisa aura sent a tingle through her. Every time she looked at this magnificent painting, she felt warmth radiate in the room and a profound stillness cocooned her. Her father's brush stroke captured her faint smile as Viola remembered.

The police officer shut the door behind him for their private meeting.

'I have the largest group of artists this time around, ten in total. Wonderful talented artists! Beautiful folk!'

His voice dropped, he looked away.

'Last night one of them disappeared with no explanations leaving us in a quandary on what happened to him.'

'Papa, what do you mean *disappeared*?' Viola's wild interjection switched over to her investigator's head.

'People do not just disappear without a reason. Have you checked with the artist's family or associates? Do you collect those details when you select artists for your program?'

Her barrage of questions confused his tired mind, he paused to sift through what to answer first.

'His room reveals nothing, no struggle, no forced entry, it appears he just left. The strange thing is all his belongings are still in the cottage.'

Viola studied her father's face, hoping to gain some understanding of what was going through his mind to help her make sense of the strange situation.

'Surely papa, he must have spoken to someone in residence?'

'Nobody knows, I checked every room, spoke to all nine artists. I hit a brick wall and had to call the police. You know creatives, Artista, never close to, or personal with anyone. I could not trace any contact person to understand why this happened. All my artists are in a state of shock. Creative energy is low with the stress this has caused. These are good people. They did not pack up and run off.'

'I am so sorry to hear this. I hope we find out soon what happened. You cannot get ill over this, as much as I know that you care deeply about the people you invite here, but you cannot neglect yourself.'

Viola understood that her father's past, the disappearance of his sister, Lorenza, had come back to haunt him. He never got over her disappearance. Years rolled on and his pain settled into a gnawing numbness. Creative expression helped him during his depressive bouts when emotions overshadowed rational judgement. The situation now at Galleria Bardo brought renewed fear that confused and unsettled him.

'I worry when the tabloids get hold of this, and they will, they will crucify me! That will mark the end of the gallery. Who will want to come here if they perceive it to be a dangerous place? And I might get blamed for poor security. I cannot stop these wild thoughts. Will you work with the police to unravel this?'

'I am worried about you, and no, I cannot get involved with the police, you know that papa. I wish I could...'

They spoke for an hour until the police officer tapped on the door.

'Mr Bardo, I need a word with you.'

Her father shot her an anxious look. She stepped out the room and whispered she would be back after his meeting.

'Artista, please check on my artists, tell them I will see them later this afternoon.'

Her room in the main cottage was tidy and ready for her whenever she visited. It overlooked the cluster of cottages that artists on site made their home for however long they stayed. Some came in for a week or two for the artists' in-residence program, and some stayed on for an extra week as her father's special guests. His generosity was his downfall. He was a man easily exploited by hard-luck stories. Yet another bone of contention for her mother during the warring years of their marriage. He had a small staff these days, a driver and general assistant to maintain the buildings and grounds. His glorious former years with a staff of thirty, lavish dinners, and his artist friends hanging around for creative respite — now gone.

Galleria Bardo was a shadow of its golden years.

Yet the spirit of the place was unchanged, for Viola at any rate. It was a warm and inviting home. She showered, donned her satin kaftan hanging in the cupboard, as she had left it a year ago, and strolled down to the general workroom.

She was not expecting to see anyone at work after what happened the night before. Her father revealed that creativity had halted in the wake of the artist's unexplained departure.

A young man stood over his easel, lost in the sway and rhythm of his brush. She peered from behind him. His canvas reflected a couple poised in a waltz with a child watching on. What captivated Viola was the intensity in the couple's eyes. The young artist created passion and adoration in the posture and penetrating eyes of the couple. A soft light bathed them with the child in the upper left quadrant looking down, spellbound by the dancing pair.

Suddenly the artist sensed her presence and turned.

'I'm sorry to disturb you. Your work is amazing! I cannot

stop looking at the couple. You are telling a story, aren't you? I can't wait to see the finished piece.'

Viola gushed and kicked herself when the artist responded with a blank stare.

'I'll slip out quietly and leave you to it.'

'No, mademoiselle, please stay.'

His soft, lilting accent sent a ripple of goosebumps down her arms and legs.

'Are you sure? I'm Viola Bar...'

His boyish face broke into a huge grin.

'Monsieur Placido's daughter! He told us you were arriving from Athens today.'

He reached out for her hand and kissed it with a reverence she felt she did not deserve. Viola's light-headedness triggered either by the delightful artist before her or the stress of her arrival, had her opt for the artist's swoon-worthy effect. Chivalry set her heart apace. Here was a boy, perhaps around twenty-five, with the face of a handsome mythological god, kissing her hand!

'I am Lamar. Please excuse my messy hands.'

'I am quite used to messy hands! Being around my father prepared me well.'

She laughed and saw the brilliant smile pass over Lamar's handsome face again.

'From Australia, I believe?'

'Yes, I see my father has revealed all!'

'Your father, he is proud of you.'

'My overindulgent wonderful, father! He asked me to let you, and the other artists know that he will see you all later this afternoon.'

'I look forward to seeing him.'

'Sad news about your peer, but he will return.'

A cloud of sadness passed over Lamar's bright, curious eyes.

'Merci, I hope so.'

She left Lamar to his work, awkward with what else she could say to comfort him when she knew nothing about the missing artist.

Viola paused at the gallery entrance to stare up at the life-size painting of her aunt Lorenza. Her father took three years to complete the masterpiece and turned down all awards. It was his tribute to his beloved sister, and he refused to put a price tag on her memory. The office door opened and her father emerged alone.

'How was your meeting, papa?'

'I'll tell you about it soon, have you had anything to eat yet? Let's go to the kitchen?'

The kitchen and dining hall for artists was at the rear of the property. Viola recalled the bustling years when elaborate meals were prepared to feed starving artists. Wine flowed and laughter echoed in the courtyard. Today it was quiet and empty, but a wonderful, familiar, spicy aroma wafted up her nostrils.

'Madalena is preparing meals for us this week and promised she would come in every morning while you are here. She has been loyal to me through the years.'

'That is her chicken peri-peri I smell. My goodness, I have not seen her in a long time!'

Madalena, Placido's youngest cousin, was the only family that stood by him during his lean years. She was ten years older than Viola. Her hearing impairment after a viral infection halted her music career as a skillful pianist. She relied on vibration to guide her new compositions. The only time she played was at the gallery. When things were good, Placido paid her well, and sent her to the best doctors and specialists. Her hearing improved for brief spells making ongoing medical treatment unaffordable.

'Is Madalena in the kitchen?'

'No, Artista, she will be back in the morning and sends her love to you.'

'I look forward to seeing her tomorrow. Now, what did the police want when they asked for a private meeting?'

'It's the same thing over-and-over again, did I see or hear anything, can I recall anything to help them. I know nothing more than what I said last night, but they look at me expecting something new. Then they tell me, unless they have a body, a dead one, or a report of a missing person from next of kin, they cannot proceed with an investigation. Can you believe that?'

Placido's breathlessness alarmed her. His anxiety had escalated.

'Please slow down, papa.'

'I'll be fine. Anyway, how about you? Did everything go well in Athens? Was the outcome as expected?'

'I suppose it did.'

Placido knew that Viola would not say anything on the specifics of her investigative work in Athens, and he respected her privacy. He needed her now to be his comfort and listening ear — his lighthouse and anchor.

He poured himself a glass of red wine and offered her a glass.

'Green tea is what I need, papa. I will make myself a cup. You should try some.'

'Tea and a green one for me? You are joking meu filho! Wine is my fine choice, thank you,' he chuckled, 'always the healthy choice, like Lorenza. She left her mark on you for sure.'

His wistful, drooped lips told her it was time to change the topic.

'I'm here to make sure you are eating nutritious food. Have you been taking care of yourself?'

She shook her head and tapped his round belly.

'It's called aging, we all go that way! I wish I had this body in my younger years, then maybe, just maybe, your mother would not have left me! She complained that I was too skinny. Her husband, the dancing maths professor, has quite a gut too!'

He looked at his Artista with a cheeky twinkle in his tired eyes and left for the workroom to check on the artists.

THAT NIGHT while Viola slept dead to the world, Placido tossed and turned replaying the last twenty-four hours.

2

The artists' workroom door was ajar. Everything inside appeared as they had left it yesterday. Placido was in quiet conversation with someone. At the end of the room, next to the French doors, stood Lamar's large painting of the dancing couple and child. Across the image, defacing its charm, a smeared, gigantic red, X sucked Viola's breath. She tried to decode the omen, but was unfamiliar with the artist, and could not understand it.

Placido called out to her when he saw her.

'Dear merciful God! Lamar has gone! Look at his painting. It's ruined!'

Viola rushed across the room to her father. His agitation was marked in his raised voice.

'Papa, please sit down, may I get you a glass of water?'

He lifted his hand in protest, lost for words, shaking his head in disbelief.

'Tell me about Lamar, help me understand. I met him briefly so nothing makes sense.'

'Nothing makes sense, you're right. Not Lamar! What a

soft, and gentle person, why is this happening? Voltaire, now Lamar! Both gone!'

'Perhaps Lamar left for a walk, maybe to get a coffee?'

'No, we commit to no outside interactions during the in-residence contract period. I only consider emergencies after a stringent questioning process. The days here are sacred to the craft. Artists must fully embrace the energy Galleria Bardo provides.'

Viola heard for the first time that her easy going father ran a tight creative ship. She paced the room, searching for other clues of perhaps forced entry to destroy Lamar's work. With emotions tossed aside, her investigative head took control, scanning, and scrutinizing every item in the workroom. The cluttered space had paints, brushes, blank canvases stacked against the walls, and fresh paintings laid out on a large wooden table. It was a room that exuded frenzied activity in the grip of creative inspiration.

'Papa, before we alert the police it is imperative that you check with the artists and Lamar's contacts, family or friends if they have heard from him.'

'You know artists, for heavens sakes you have lived with this one your entire life! We like solitude. I don't know, but I will check the records.'

During this time, the young female artist her father spoke with, stepped aside, hovering at the entrance, listening to the conversation between them.

'Artista, this is Ariel. She and Lamar worked well together this week. Both are brilliant surrealist artists. Ariel, this is my daughter, Viola.'

Ariel tried to smile, but Viola saw fear scalding her eyes. Lost and unsure. A slight figure, more boyish with her pixie features and close-cropped hair. Her pallor depicted one who spent many hours indoors. Viola hoped she could find answers to help them both understand what happened to Lamar.

'I don't know… what to think… I can't make sense of this…' Ariel stammered.

'This is Lamar's painting. I saw him working on it.'

'Err… yes… but when I last saw it,… it did not have the red cross smudged on it.'

Placido stared out the French doors.

'We have to be hopeful, there has to be a logical reason which we cannot seem to find right now. Papa, please check for any contact details you have for Lamar. This seems like a matter for the police. The painting sends a sinister warning. You also need to ask the officer on watch if there was unusual activity late last night.'

Placido left the workroom and Viola turned to Ariel, hoping she would speak up on what she was thinking and feeling.

'Ariel, this is a great shock to you as it is to my father. Can you tell me what you know about Lamar? The police will ask you this question and you must be clear about what you know.'

Her wide, darting eyes and flaming red ears against her alabaster face, softened Viola's probing.

'I know nothing, please, we spoke about art most of the time…'

'That is fine, so he shared nothing about his personal life with you?'

'No.'

Placido returned graver than when he left.

'All I have on record is his neighbor's telephone number. She is an elderly woman, quite deaf. I had to raise the roof before she knew what I was on about. She has not seen him nor heard from him since he left two weeks ago.'

'No other contacts, papa, are you sure about that?'

'Absolutely, no other details.'

'Alert the officer on shift and make an official statement at the police station as soon as possible.'

'I will do that now. You and Ariel should have a glass of wine. I need one to steady my nerves.'

'Not now papa! You cannot have alcohol on your breath when you go down to the police station. Speak to the police officer outside first.'

Ariel wanted a glass of water. Viola was relieved with her sensible choice.

Placido invited the police officer into his office.

'I have nothing much to report except that Ariel and I confirm that Lamar has disappeared. I called his neighbor, but she has not seen him for a while. I don't know what to do with another artist gone!'

The officer studied Placido's body language. His fidgeting fingers and hesitant eyes did him no favors.

'He said nothing to this, er… Ariel?'

'No, that's what she says. His artwork is something you should see. It unnerves me. Something is afoot and we need urgent action. I fear for our safety.'

'Mr Bardo, stay here, do not go down to the station. I will make a record of what you are reporting to me. It is too early to guess that what happened the other night is related to today's incident. Your safety is a priority. Stay put today. We must determine if there is a connection between the two artists who have disappeared. Can you think of anything that might be a link between them?'

'Apart from the fact that they are artists, one a surrealist painter and the other a cubist, both highly skilled artists, silent, deep types, that is all I can tell you. But the red marking across Lamar's painting is baffling.'

'Do you have any known enemies who would try to hurt you this way, Mr Bardo?'

'What are you trying to say? How is this tied to me?'

'I'm asking to make sense of what might have provoked this situation at Galleria Bardo, or whether it is an external issue. Please do not take it personally. Two artists mysteriously missing from the same location is an odd occurrence. You would have to agree, Mr Bardo.'

'How can I not take it personally? And yes, it is odd. These are artists I handpicked to join my residence program.'

'I understand, but you will be called to report all you know about them from the first day you met the artists.'

'I have reported this to your chief and will wait for instructions. I should let Ariel and my daughter know that I have spoken to you and that you advise that I do not go down to the station now. Do you think I should let my attorney know about this?'

'Up to you, Mr Bardo. If I were you, sir, I would get legal support right away.'

The officer's words rang with a hollowness that sent a searing ache through Placido's chest. He took a deep breath and walked out the office to find Viola waiting at the door.

'I have to call my attorney. The officer thinks police will be watching me in all of this. Meu filho, why, why has this happened?'

'Papa, keep your emotions in check, please. We cannot have you ill, now, that will raise a false suspicion.'

Placido lived life through his emotions. The highs and lows were the seat of his best works.

Viola knew her father had packed on the pounds since she last saw him a year ago. His breathing was raspy, and profuse perspiration moistened the armpits and neckline of his flowing blue shirt on this cool morning.

'I will try, Artista. You know I live between the extremes of calm and passion.'

'I am here now so I will keep you in check. The last thing you want is for police to speculate on your involvement because of your irrational reactions. Then they will hook their claws into you. Stay strong in your truth, papa. That is how you raised me, remember?'

'I am so glad you are here, meu filho, so glad.'

Both did not expect the swift decisions police made that morning.

* * *

THE MORNING PASSED in quiet unease. Eight remaining artists heeded Placido's advice to stay indoors in their cottages. The workroom was now a crime scene. Handpicked artists from Portugal, France, South Africa, and India chose Galleria Bardo because they valued Placido's craft, the supremacy of his artistry. Placido Bardo's noted works, cited in international artistic journals, and featured in Time magazine, positioned him as an artist who crossed genres from modernist to contemporary art. The global refugee crisis, captured in a heart-wrenching painting, gained him the illustrious global Marquis Award. He was dubbed a Dali-Monet-Warhol in his experimentation with genre. His *Bardoesque* paintings featured women as dominant figures.

After the chief of police called at the gallery, Viola had to move out of her father's home while the investigation was in progress. Her arrival after the disappearance of the first artist, and her presence during second disappearance, were deemed as complicating matters for the police.

She knew they wanted to put the screws on her father and saw her as his protector.

Viola secured an Airbnb in the city center and would have to find casual work to pay for the accommodation she had not built into her holiday budget. As the taxi drove out of the entrance of her father's gallery, the signpost at the gate tugged at her.

All who enter through the gates of Galleria Bardo never leave untouched.

This dual sided entry and parting sign depicted her father's passion, but she knew his propensity to accept blame for everything that went awry in his world. His divorce from Helena, his sister Lorenza's disappearance and now this... Leaving him on his own during this crisis made her restless.

Sleep toyed with her in this strange apartment. She scoured the internet hoping to find some information on the two missing artists. They either did not have social media accounts or had erased them. She found newspaper and journal articles on the artistic prowess of Lamar and the older artist Voltaire — both from France. She pondered whether that might be the connection to aiding the search for them. Viola remembered the carefree days she spent at her father's gallery home. People came and went as they pleased. Now everything was under watch or forbidden. What had her father neglected as due diligence when he interviewed the artists for his residency program?

Lamar was in his twenties, but Voltaire was pushing fifty. Voltaire had come to Galleria Bardo hoping to summon a second wind of creativity. That was as much as her father could tell her. She found another link to Voltaire online. He appeared to have been selling his works at a flea market in Paris. No documented proof suggested a struggle that toppled his glorious years. Her father erred in trusting without checking. Mounting financial burdens and age made him negligent.

She jumped out of bed. Her head buzzed with all the

scenarios she imagined on what could have happened at the gallery. The apartment had a microwave, bar fridge, a kettle, and a tiny stove top with no oven. The temptation to bake at this hour would not be possible. She craved a piece of peanut brittle but had none. A morning trot to the shops might lead to finding some. Her skittish energy needed work to contain it. She had limited funds after her stint at Aurora Academy, and could barely pay the rent here, but she would never dream of asking her father for help. An inner voice advised that she should call Rob Dwyer in Sydney. She did not envision being back at Blackwater Ridge for term one of the new year.

A newspaper on the coffee table caught her attention. It was a day old, perhaps the positions advertised were still available. She paged through and found nothing suitable. A supermarket check-out job is a position she might take on. Then her eye caught the tiny advertisement for an English teaching position at an adult college. She applied online. It was a part-time position for two evening classes per week. The pay was good to cover rent and food. That was all she needed.

Her phone buzzed and cut off before she could pick up the call. The hasty caller was unlisted. Could it be Tempest? She was the only one who called from a private number.

3

With no contact number to trace the caller, Viola was restless and careless about her body's signs. Her light-headed spells were frequent, and her coffee intake increased. While her father's situation hung in the balance, her wellness crumbled. She strolled onto the high street looking for a confectionery store with peanut brittle, and chastised herself for her addiction. As a smoker craved a puff, the peanut crunch and caramel juice soothed her fraught nerves.

Her phone rang again. She dived to retrieve the unidentified call, compelled by curiosity.

'I'm so glad you picked up, Ms Bardo.'

Viola's head grew lighter when she heard the familiar but unexpected voice on the other end. Her toes curled into a tight ball and blood rushed to her head.

Matthew Soto was on the line to her barely a week after she left Athens. She panicked, perhaps something had happened to the child. Had he lost custody of the boy? Why was he calling her? He said he would be in touch, but not this soon.

'Hello, Matthew? This is a surprise. How are you, Jungen and Bernice?'

'Ah, so good to know you recognized my voice! We are well, thank you. How are you? Having a wonderful reunion with your father?'

Viola heard the delight and relief in his voice. She was not at liberty to reveal the happenings at the gallery even though the media would soon devour the story, sensationalize it, and heaven forbid, demonize her father.

'Yes, yes, it is lovely to be with my father after all this time.'

In awkward situations, she veered towards formality.

'Have I caught you in a busy moment? If so, tell me the best time to call back.'

'I was on my way out, but I can chat for a few minutes.'

She had to create urgency as she sensed his intensity before she left Athens. He unnerved and excited her.

'I called as late as I could, hoping you would be available for a conversation. I have been thinking it might be good for Jungen to see you again... soon. If you can fit in a visit from us, we can come over to Portugal, make a holiday of it and see you at the same time?'

Viola held her breath. Why did this have to be uncomfortable? He could have made a friendly call without imposing on her. Was it really his concern that the child needed to see her or his need? Jungen had spent just one day with her in Athens, and a fleeting visit thereafter amidst the chaos of his situation. She had to respond quickly without upsetting him. In the background, her memory lurked on Tempest's warning that Matthew had a violent temper. Something she never experienced nor suspected in her previous interactions with him. That he was a persistent man, she accepted.

'Now is not a good time, I'm afraid. I would love to see you both… three… but I am not quite settled here… yet, and busy helping my father settle a few matters.'

Her ears were on fire, her brow damp as she waited for his reaction.

Silence on the other end.

Viola pressed her lips together, afraid to breathe because she was stretching the truth. Matthew's training in the military meant he could sniff out fabrications or half-truths in an instant. She stood up, paced around the small apartment, waiting for Matthew Soto to respond.

Then his characteristic deep sigh.

'I understand, Ms Bardo, sorry to have disturbed you with your hectic schedule. Another time, perhaps? Have a lovely Christmas.'

He was off the line before she could respond. Viola kicked the coffee table, frustrated with this complication that arrived uninvited.

Now was not a good time for anything.

Matthew held an appeal she did not want to entertain. The chance that he would call again appeared dismal.

Her phone rang again.

'Matthew? Look…'

'Viola, Sebastian, here. Is Matthew still in touch with you?'

She cringed for her stupidity in not checking her phone before she picked up the call. What if it was her father? She would have to explain who Matthew was, and she was not prepared to do that.

'Why are you calling from a private number? Did you call earlier?'

'Wow! Happy to hear your voice too, Viola! It was just a prank. Sorry, I should call another time.'

'Oh! Dear God, I am sorry Sebastian. My morning has kicked off to a terrible start.'

'Has Matthew Soto upset you?'

'Not really, he wants to come over with Jungen and I told him it was not a good time, now I think he's upset with me.'

Sebastian paused, tried to digest what he was hearing. It sounded like a domestic situation between the two.

'You are free to do as you please without worrying about how Soto feels. Or dare I ask, are you in love with this man?'

'Don't be ridiculous, Sebastian!'

'Forget I asked. How are things down Porto way?'

She hesitated. Should she tell him what had happened at the gallery?

'It's going well, papa is busy with his artists' workshops, so I decided to book into an Airbnb and will join him once they have left.'

Her words flowed with the ease of a pathological liar. It was her papa, and she had to protect him until she knew how to help him.

'I see, I want to invite you over to New York, the next time you have a break, or you could take on some exchange work here. I can arrange that.'

What was with these newfound men in her life — all wanted to crowd her space, barely giving her time to think!

'That is kind of you, but it will take a lot of planning and I will have to feel out my situation when I get back to Australia. Rob Dwyer might think it time to hire someone else in my position. His kindness might run out, with my frequent vacating of the position, you know.'

All she had to ask was how things were upon his return to classes and he droned on about his students and the puppy he took in from the local pound and how hectic his life was. She closed her eyes and listened with as much patience as she could. Sebastian was a lonely soul, and it would be unkind not to listen to him. He had no idea she had walked into a minefield of mysterious circumstances that placed her father at great peril. Now was not the right time to tell him, or anyone outside the gallery anything.

After Sebastian hung up, she made a pot of tea and peanut butter toast with a drizzle of honey. The rental agency provided a hospitality basket with just the things she loved. Peanut butter and honey were as close as she was going to get to peanut brittle!

* * *

She slept in longer than expected. An email arrived overnight checking if she was available for an interview at the adult college. The person leaving had taken ill. Viola needed the job and accepted the interview. It was at 10 am. She had an hour to get ready.

Her city apartment was in an ideal location for a quick coffee from the cafe outside the apartment and to grab an ever ready cab. This time she was relaxed about the interview, unlike her interview with Matthew Soto for the au pair position. If she got the college position, her hunt for temporary work was over to free her to investigate things at Galleria Bardo. She leaned back in the cab and looked at her phone.

A message from her father worried her.

Call me as soon as you can Artista

She hoped he had good news and would call him after her interview.

The interview was a breeze, but one requirement for the position was to be available for the duration of the summer until the course had ended. There were no interviews lined up after her, and the position was hers. All she had to do was sign to accept and start. She had twenty-four hours to ponder if this was the right fit for her. Her priority was a call to Rob Dwyer at an appropriate time. An email would be impersonal. She shared a special relationship with her Australian headmaster and had much to be grateful for in his leniency with allowing her to come and go with an assured position when she returned to home soil. This was something she had to be mindful of, kindness, if not returned, had an expiry date.

How she wished she could pop over to Galleria Bardo to see her father. She had to remain within the law, and a telephone call was all the police permitted until they lifted her ban. At one forty-five, she called her father.

'Papa, I'm so sorry I could not call sooner. I was in an interview...'

Her father's anguished voice made her belly somersault.

'Artista, things have got worse, Ariel has gone! Now the police want to question me at the central police station!'

'What? You are not a suspect! I am coming to the station to be with you. What time are you going in?'

'No, please I don't want any trouble for you, they have forbidden you to see me.'

'The police did not instruct me not to see you outside the gallery. If they want technicalities, I have one!'

A sudden clicking sound made the call a tad crackly.

'Papa? Are you there?'

'Yes, I am. Please be careful. I am so worried for you.'

Viola sensed someone was listening in, and now the intruder knew she was going to the police station to meet her father. Her father's emotional state meant she had to remain quiet about the uninvited listener. She steered the conversation to a quick conclusion.

'I'll be fine, papa, what time should I meet you at the police station?'

'At three o' clock. Wait there for me.'

* * *

THE ROOM SPUN. She bent over to clear her head. All she had eaten was the peanut butter and honey toast last night and downed a coffee this morning. She poured a large glass of water and knocked it back before she headed out to the central police station. Food was not a priority today.

A female police officer escorted Viola to the waiting area to meet her father. It was five past three and he had not arrived. The female officer made a call to the interviewing team and advised Viola that Placido was picked up half an hour ago and already in the meeting room.

Viola was denied entry into the room. Her father had not contacted his attorney and now he was at the mercy of the police who felt it necessary to haul him in for further questioning. She forced her way in, announcing that her father had the right to a witness, or he would not say another word until she brought in his attorney.

The question posed when she sat behind her father was designed to irk her.

'What is your involvement with the three missing artists who trusted you when they signed up for your residency program?'

Her father shook his head. His voice was soft and trembling.

'I am not involved in this, I have no reason to do this and am worried sick for their safety.'

'Why is their safety a concern? You seem to know that there is some risk to them.'

Viola felt every nerve pulsating for an outburst, but she held it together in silence. Anything she said would jeopardize her father's situation.

'They were in my gallery, my home when this happened, I

am human. My concern is natural. Only a beast would not care.'

'Do you have any enemies who would want to hurt you?'

'I cannot answer that question because I do not know. I lead a secluded life and step on nobody's toes.'

'Tell us what you know about the three missing artists.'

'I have already answered this question. They are talented artists. One joined the residency to rekindle his passion. I only have what is on their application forms and accompanying resumes.'

'We shall have those removed from your office later this afternoon.'

'It is private information but if it will help in finding them then by all means, take it.'

'Just one more thing, Mr Bardo, we have to detain you tonight in the wake of what has happened on three consecutive nights at your gallery.'

Viola could not hold back another minute.

'My father has a right to an attorney. Why is this necessary if there is no evidence to prove his guilt?'

'My dear Ms Bardo, this is to clear your father, not prosecute him. An attorney is unnecessary at this point.'

'It is my father's legal right to have an attorney. Papa, please give me the details. I will call your attorney.'

The officer questioning her father was not someone she had seen at the gallery, neither was he the chief of police. Had they summoned her father under a pretext?

One way or another, she was going to find out what happened at Galleria Bardo while her father lay sleeping.

Viola's call shocked Martens Direito.

As a retired judge, he advised and acted for a small select clientele he met during his years in the justice department. For her it was verboten to entertain the thought of her father spending a night in a crummy police station, in a urine scented holding space. This could not happen to her papa, a delicate, mild-mannered man. Dare anyone try to convince her otherwise!

Martens Direito confirmed that there was no legitimate charge against Placido and that he would arrive at the central police station in an hour.

Placido was silent when she returned. Closed off, trapped in distraction. She touched his shoulder and whispered that Martens would arrive soon. He nodded and withdrew into a silent space again which she understood as the way he processed his creative energy. The female police officer looked in at the door and with a flick of her head, she motioned for Viola to step into the corridor.

'Ms Bardo, have you contacted your father's lawyer?'

'I have, why do you ask?'

'Good! Your father looks unwell, and if he is to stay here tonight who knows what could happen, you know what I mean?'

'Thank you for your concern, ma'am, I'm sure they will send him home. He is innocent.'

'Who is your father's attorney?'

Viola's suspicion made her reluctant to answer. While the questions were in consideration for her father's welfare, she doubted the intention. Her protective instinct took hold. The wall was up, yet deep down she knew she had to indulge the officer as things could go horribly wrong for Placido.

'Martens Direito.'

The officer's eyebrows raised in half-moon crescents.

'Good, he's excellent.'

Viola excused herself from further questions and stepped back inside the holding room. Placido looked at her with worry darkening his eyes.

'Artista, what did that woman want? Why were you talking to her? Where's Martens?'

'Papa, she showed concern for you. That is all.'

'Don't trust these people. Look at how they dragged me here and then did not want me to call Martens in for legal advice.'

'Martens will be here in twenty minutes. Can I get you a coffee?'

'I need something stronger like Poncha!'

'Coffee it shall be. No wine, no alcohol until all this is over, *acabado*!'

Placido laughed. Hearing Viola drop a Portuguese word here and there always delighted him. She did so when she scolded him.

'Artista you sound like your mother, but more like your aunt Lorenza, my baby sister...'

'We shall never stop missing her, for me it's an honor that you see me in her image, papa.'

'Not your mother, you think?'

His cheeky grin gave her hope that the father she loved and adored was still the same beneath the stress of all he had to endure.

At 6:30 pm a flustered and exhausted Martens Direito arrived. He got through the paperwork to have Placido released with permission granted for Viola to spend the night with him. But she had to leave the gallery residence by nine the next morning.

Getting back to Galleria Bardo was a homecoming tinged with uncertainty. It was one night, but she knew soon she would return to continue her treasured time with her father.

Placido arranged a gathering of the seven remaining artists. They had a right to know what was going on and they remained in solidarity with his innocence and their concern for the missing artists. He felt the strain of having to tell them that they could not leave, as instructed by the powers that be at the station, until there were leads on the case that did not involve them. Sensitive souls with bemused expressions were silent with their intention and mission in limbo.

Viola filled the coffee urn in the dining area, placed biscuits on a platter and hoped the artists would remain in kindred loyalty to her father as they had up to this point. A wide-eyed woman, a South African artist, was the first to break the silence.

'I am hanging onto the hope that our peers left of their own choosing. Why? That is the mystery.'

A young artist nodded for some time before he looked up at each face in the circle.

'Perhaps they were a trio, acting together in their choice to leave. It is a mystery, ma'am.'

Viola studied the faces of the two who spoke, in awe of their humility, gentle souls, prolific artists who left their countries to seek inspiration from her father. She felt a swell of pride for him. It was always there, but to see him acknowledged by people he met two short weeks ago, made her glow.

Crystal, a Pattachitra folk artist, addressed Placido in a way Viola had never heard before. Her brother Dillon, also in residence, was a mild-mannered political cartoonist.

'Revered sir, I fervently hope that this does not affect your work as an artist. We live in a strange world that judges before knowing. It is our beholden duty to diffuse this from happening.'

She looked around at her fellow artists, expecting their reactions. Five nodded in agreement and each stood up and shook Placido's hand. One remained glum and silent and the others put it down to his stress with the happenings.

After an emotionally draining day, Viola saw the tears in her father's eyes. He cleared his throat.

'That is a lovely gesture, thank you. Let us see what tomorrow brings. You are all exhausted and distressed as I am. I wish you a good night's rest and thank you once again.'

'We are here to see this through.' Crystal said to the sounds of 'oh yes, we are,' and 'absolutely.'

One by one they departed after a private word with Placido and thanked him for keeping them informed.

Viola turned on the television, poured another cup of coffee and sat on the couch close to her father.

'Too much coffee this late will steal sleep, Artista.'

'Never fear, sleep finds me regardless of the number of cups I consume,' she laughed.

'If you say so.'

'You going to be ok, papa?'

'With you beside me how can I not be anything but more than ok!'

He kissed the top of her head as he did when she was a child, afraid and sleepless.

The television news played in the background until the gallery appeared on the screen to threaten their cozy family moment. The thing that stood out was the label attached to Galleria Bardo as the place where artists mysteriously vanish.

'Turn it off, please Artista, I cannot bear to hear misrepresented news!'

Viola reached over and rubbed her father's temples.

'Papa, the media will ramp up things, so ignore it, please.'

'You are right, it's getting late, meu filho, we should go to bed. It has been a rough day. I know I won't sleep a wink worrying about the remaining artists, but we must try to rest.'

'Security at the entrance and at the back has increased so you have nothing to worry about, papa.'

'Who knows? Strange things have happened, and I don't know why.'

'No negativity now, deep breaths and a hot shower is what you need!'

'I will do that. You must promise me you will rest too.'

'I will and we can chat again in the morning before I leave.'

Placido sighed and heaved his bulky body from the couch.

Viola lay in bed awake for several hours. She pulled out her journal and wrote:

Papa dear and kind
you are a gem — a rare find
artists seek you out
your craft rare and devout

At 6 am she heard her father in the kitchen. Her phone pinged. It was Helena. Viola had no desire to read the message, but knew she had to tell her father that her mother knew about the problem at Galleria Bardo. Damn the media! She wanted details and would not back off until she got what she wanted. Helena believed that Placido was in police custody and refused to accept Viola's message to the contrary.

She told her father about her mother's speculations.

'She teaches fiction, so she lives it too. Give her the information she craves. Call her and I will speak to her, Artista.'

'Are you sure?'

'Yes, I did not sleep much but I am ready to defend my innocence.'

Viola was pleased to hear his old fighting spirit return.

'Mother. How are you? No, papa is right here beside me. He went in for a few hours of questioning.'

Placido reached for the phone.

'Helena, I am here at the gallery. I am in the dark about what has happened, so I cannot tell you much more than you would have heard on the news.'

Viola heard a high-pitched, one-sided conversation with her father's profuse utterances of thanks.

'Thanks for your concern, Helena, bye now.'

'That was brief.'

'Our entire time together was brief, Artista. I should not expect love or empathy from her, but I keep thinking she will show some care.'

'Did she say anything about me being here?'

'She said I'm lucky you are with me.'

'That's it? I should not expect more from her either.'

'Leave her to her own happiness. I am not sure why she wanted to know the details. Perhaps she does care after all.'

The sadness in his voice made Viola's heart lurch. For all the years that had passed, Helena moved on and he still lived in hope.

For Viola, love existed in poetry and her father was a living persona in John Keats' *La Belle Dame Sans Merci*.

'Forget the call, but you must remember to be cautious about what you say on the landline.'

She lowered her voice, aware that the officer at the door would crane to listen in to their conversation.

'I wish you could stay. I am going to ask Martens to request this.'

'Leave it for now, papa.'

She could not tell him she wanted to carry out her own investigation outside the gallery away from police gaze.

At 9 am on her way back to the Airbnb, she received an email asking if she had considered taking on the English college position.

5

With a teaching position settled, Viola was ready to begin in two days.

It was time to celebrate her success.

The pastry shop at the top end of her street had peanut brittle, her hunt was over, and it was a fudge-soft type, easy on her perishing teeth. She planned on stopping there whenever she needed a caramel-nut hit!

With the day to herself she strolled back to the apartment and on a whim took a detour to a side lane with intriguing murals. Her father had never mentioned this latest addition to the city's street art. It was fascinating. The images jumped out and seemed to walk alongside her. One held her attention. The background depicted a lone child on a swing. The center-ground held a gigantic eye with a well-shaped eyebrow, but it was the sadness in the eye that moved her. It was as real as looking into a living person's face. The foreground was a large glistening tear drop threatening to roll down the wall. The child was overshadowed by the dominance of the eye and teardrop.

What story was the artist telling? She stood before it, contemplating the message and reached into her bag for her poetry journal.

> *What sadness do you hide*
> *behind that mournful eye?*
> *little one in blue*
> *why are you lost and alone?*

Someone shuffled into the lane and stopped behind her. The shadow cast on the silvery teardrop unnerved her. Viola stepped aside to offer the person a clear view.

'Sorry.'

'Do you like it that much that you are writing about what you see?'

The voice was soft yet challenging.

She turned around to a round-bellied man with a pepper speckled beard and matching head of hair. A chill ran through her. His eyes had a startling similarity to the eye in the mural. She cleared her throat and turned back to the mural.

'Are you the artist?'

'Why do you ask?'

The soft voice grew hard.

'No reason, just a conversation starter,' she giggled with unease.

'Ah, curiosity.'

'I suppose. It is an amazing painting that captured my attention.'

'Found a connection?'

That brief, hanging line sent a shudder through her.

'Not really, pardon me, I have to dash.'

'So soon?'

Viola walked out the lane in a running step, flagged a passing taxi to grab a quick dinner from the 7 Eleven, and hurry back to her apartment. The strange encounter disturbed her, ruining her stroll around the city.

Her microwaved tasteless dinner made her desperate to begin her teaching position sooner. Money was tight and tapping into her Australian savings was not an option she could afford. It was time to let Rob Dwyer know that she might not be back at Blackwater Ridge Performing Arts in time for the new term. Requesting extra leave was something she did all the time, yet this time she was uncomfortable with asking. It was more that she was going to tell her headmaster that she was not coming back as expected. It was unfair to breeze in for half a term and put someone out because of her erratic schedule. Calling him was out of the question. He would try to persuade her to return or promise that he would hold a mid-term position for her. An email it had to be. It was the summer break in Australia, and Rob, being Rob, would be in his office planning staffing allocations for the new year. She had to get to it right away.

Dear Mr Dwyer,

I hope this finds you well and not too exhausted from the end-of-year activities.

I am sorry to advise that I cannot return for term one and know you are putting in allocations now for next year and had to get this to you as soon as possible. Something has come up and I cannot leave my father anytime soon. It is better that I clear this now as I envision, I will have to be around until things improve.

If you can fit me in, I will return in term two. But as always, I do not expect special consideration.

I apologize for this change to my original plan when I left Blackwater Ridge. It is beyond my control.

I wish you and yours a blessed Christmas and hope you can find time to relax.

Take care,
Kindest regards,
Viola Bardo

She hovered the cursor over the send button, sighed and hit it. It pained her but was necessary to allow Rob to plan for the upcoming year. No amount of over thinking was going to change things. Her father and Galleria Bardo needed her. It was not possible to provide Rob with any details on her reason for delaying her return to Australia. He would worry and want to call her. She hoped he would reply by email and not insist on a telephone conversation. This was not the night for a guilt trip. She picked up her novel, snuggled into the couch, and lost herself in the pages of a political saga.

Two hours later, the persistent beeping of her cell phone ended her journey into another world.

'Up for a chat, Ms Bardo?' Sebastian chirped on the line.

'Hey, Sebastian, do you mean, with you?' She taunted, and then slipped in, 'anytime!'

'Jeez, you had me worried there, you tease!'

'To what do I owe this honor?'

'Can't a friend call with no specific reason?'

'Come on, now, stop being sensitive,' she laughed, 'guess what, I have secured a teaching post so I will be here for a while longer than I had planned.'

'Is that the college you spoke of when we last chatted! Congratulations!'

'Yes, it is, two nights a week.'

'How do you feel about teaching adults as opposed to teenagers?'

'I think the change will do me a world of good. I am reaching out of my comfort zone, I know, with teaching English. Not sure if I mentioned that the last time.'

'Wow! You are cutting a different path there! I admire your verve.'

'You would do the same if you were bordering on being cashless! Vigilante work is a frugal life, agent Sebastian!'

'You have your father to help you out, right? And how is your Aussie headmaster taking the news?'

'I don't know yet, I sent him an email. My father is in a bit of a financial pickle these days, so I will not ask for any favors, or tell him about my financial situation.'

'Look, Viola, I'm going to cut to the chase, we are skirting around issues. I saw the news here on what has happened at Galleria Bardo. It is not a secret if the world knows.'

'News spreads as we sleep, this reminds me of something Mark Twain said, *A lie can travel halfway around the world while truth is putting on its shoes.* What exactly do you know?'

'Forget that, is your father OK?'

'So, my father is being scandalized in the news, is he?'

Sebastian knew he had to be careful with his choice of words.

'No, I don't believe everything I read or see on the news as Mr Twain also said, that with the newspaper you are uninformed if you don't read it and then misinformed when you do! That is my thinking too. This must be a very strained time for you both.'

'It is. The police have ordered me to move out of his home while the investigation is on, but I plan to do my own sleuthing.'

'That's ridiculous! Your father is not a suspect.'

'Oh, police think he has some involvement based on nothing!'

'Viola, you need your head, it is difficult not to get emotional, but your papa needs your help. While I am on that, I have a message from Tempest.'

'Tempest? I haven't heard from her, and I cannot take on anything now.'

'It's not a fresh case. She wants to assist with what's happened at Galleria Bardo.'

'Dear God, the news has traveled. I should have known when my mother called. Why did Tempest not contact me directly?'

'She said it is a personal matter and she cannot approach you, but to let you know if you require help, you are to send her an email. Then she will call you on when and how she will intervene through her contacts.'

'Yeah, Tempest plays by the rules. Thank you for letting me know.'

'Have a think about it, don't feel pressured to reach out to her. If you want her ever changing contact number, I can send that to you. Only do what makes you comfortable. You and your father need help from people you can trust.'

Viola blinked, Sebastian the newcomer, in her role with Tempest, was now her negotiator. She knew he had her interest at heart, but things had slanted in favor of him and a tinge of envy surfaced that she was helpless and at his mercy.

'I will think about it and let you know. What are you getting up to these days?'

She cut him off. Her emotions were raw, and she was not ready to invite anyone into the intimate details of her father's worries.

'Marking semester papers, drowning in them to be honest. You rest and email Tempest only if you feel you need help.'

Viola tossed thoughts on whether her father would reject outside help. If she accepted Tempest's offer, it would be her secret. Police investigation would drag on for months with the crazy belief that there was no urgency if there was no homicide. Her father needed his peace restored, and she would do whatever was within her power to achieve it.

At 5 am after a sleepless night she sent Sebastian a message asking for Tempest's latest contact number. He replied that Tempest had just picked up her email and would call her.

The tense waiting began.

Two hours later there was no call from Tempest.

She called Placido for the latest news on the gallery front.

'Good morning, papa, did you sleep well?'

'Oh Artista, I expect it is the same with you, no sleep at all. Thinking and more thinking, questioning all night long why and who? But at least no incidents during the night to face in the morning.'

'I am happy all was quiet last night except your busy mind traveling inside your head!'

'True, meu filho. Is the place where you are staying comfortable?'

'It's not home and I would rather be with you but it is bearable. By the way, I have a job two evenings a week at the English college. I am staying on for three months!'

'Artista! Are you sure? What about your teaching job in Australia?'

'I have it under control.'

Her emails were unchecked. She had yet to find out how Rob reacted to her prolonged time away.

'I am going to ask Martens to get you back here. You are my family and you are visiting me, so why must they send you away. I am not guilty of anything!'

'Don't get upset, papa. Yes, talk to Martens and see what

comes of it. If they do not allow it, I will ask if I can visit you a few times in the week and if police want to be present while I see you, so be it.'

'Martens must get you here for Christmas, I will insist he pulls all stops on that.'

'That would be wonderful, I have been looking forward to that for so long.'

'I am keeping my hopes up that the missing artists will return. You have a lovely day. I'm calling Martens right now.'

Viola was pleased her father sounded in control of what he wanted. Christmas was a special time for him in wanting a memorable part of their family life recalled, when Lorenza was with them.

6

Hunger pangs had Viola venturing out to the patisserie for a ham and cheese croissant. She was up for the challenge to anyone who questioned her on why Portugal had the best coffee in the world! A cup of *Sical* or *Buondi* I was her taste of heaven. Her hope of attending a barista course was dashed.

It was a beautiful warm morning with not a cloud in the sky, a rarity since her arrival in the city. Porto was easy to get around on foot, and glorious weather made it a day for walking. The spectacular view of the Duoro, colorful buildings, and small winding streets lined with cafes added to the intrigue in this perfect vacation destination. This riverside city oozed people charm, and the surroundings ignited romantic and creative desires. She could live here. It was her second home to Australia in her adult years.

With a croissant and coffee in hand, she sat on a riverside bench, inhaled the morning air in a deep long breath, and said a silent prayer for peace to return to her father. She bit into the croissant when her cell phone rang. Viola chewed as fast as she could as she rummaged in her bag for her phone, anxious when she saw an unknown number, knowing this could be Tempest.

'Viola! It's me again so soon!'

Tempest's unmistakable husky voice wafted down her ear, making her coffee and croissant morning that much better.

'Lovely to hear from you!'

She was nervous this time, her heart was too close to the problem. She dusted the pastry flakes from her jacket.

'I could call back later. You must be having breakfast.'

Considerate, knowing Tempest, either sensed Viola's awkwardness or heard her loud chewing!

'I am out at the river but can talk to you now.'

'It's better to chat when you are less distracted by the beauty around you. May I call you in an hour?'

'Yes, sure that would be better, I agree.'

Viola relaxed, relishing her takeaway breakfast before her brisk trot along the river back to her apartment. Her sixth sense picked up a gaze from across the boardwalk — there, leaning against a wall was the stranger she met at the laneway mural. He looked away when she caught his eye.

Charming, just what she did not need this morning when everything seemed perfect. She stepped up her pace, anxious and eager to make herself invisible to the stranger. Viola mastered being able to shake off situations that created fear. The one thing she failed to recover from was her inability to get behind the wheel of a car without fear or guilt overcoming her. When her safety was compromised in Athens, she jumped into survival mode in her manic drive back to Aurora College.

This stranger had no hold over her.

Metropolitan transport in Australia was swift and reliable. Here, while most places could be reached on foot, it was not possible with the art gallery being further away from the city hub. Her car remained cobwebbed in her apartment lock-up garage, close to Blackwater Ridge Performing Arts, waiting for her courage to return. After her daring driving stint in Athens, she considered plucking up the nerve to start driving again when she returned to Blackwater.

Right on cue, Tempest called in an hour.

She had to compose herself. It was her papa she had to protect. The disturbing thought was whether there was a vendetta against him.

'It's almost Christmas and the reason you're there is to have a good time with your father. I am so sorry for the problem he is facing.'

Tempest put it out there, and Viola had an obligation to respond. She choked. Tempest knew her as one in control of any situation that came her way. Now was not the time to reveal her weaker side.

She drew a quick breath and fanned her face before she spoke.

'Thank you. I am confused and do not know where to begin. The police are handling things, but I feel this will drag on for months. They are scrutinizing my father, with no grounds to do so.'

'I know it is a tough situation to investigate undercover, and on your own. With your permission may I tap into a few leads through my contacts there. As always, I guarantee your anonymity.'

Viola's shoulders dropped with relief.

'It would be great to have a few leads, thank you.'

'I cannot promise anything soon, but I can feel out the situation there. You do what you must, and I will get back to you once I have something concrete to report. Talk soon.'

The sudden silence on Tempest's end signaled she had left the conversation. Tempest, warm, caring, and abrupt at the same time.

The spoken contract between them was in motion. This time the case was in her personal zone, and her emotions were unpredictable.

* * *

THE FIRST NIGHT at the city college made Viola edgy. Her Portuguese was far from adequate to sustain communication with native speakers. The initial interview was nothing like she had ever experienced. It was as if the college only needed proof that she was human.

The head of the college met her in the foyer. She was not present at Viola's strange interview and requested to meet half an hour before her class.

A tall, gangly woman jerked her way towards Viola in slow zombie-like motion. Her bright blue eyes were a striking contrast to her red rush of hair. She extended her skinny arm, which seemed to hang from a dislodged hinge on her shoulder.

Viola smiled and froze when she received a chilly attitude from this fifty-something new boss woman.

'Viola Bardo, so we meet. I'm Vanessa Smythe, college principal.'

Her deep voice and stiff countenance suited her peculiar gait.

Viola reached out for a handshake.

'Thank you for meeting me, Ms Smythe.'

'The interview panel were impressed with you, and we have been together for enough years for me to trust their decisions.'

Viola hoped this was a thawing sign.

'That's good to know.'

She prayed the awkward conversation would not drag on for a full thirty minutes.

'Do you have any questions? I am aware you are a music teacher, so I assume you might find the first session a little strained. As you know, we are not teaching this lot academic English so that should not be daunting for you. Just the everyday ordinary sort of English.'

Every day and *ordinary* was not what she expected to hear from the head of the college and now it was too late to ask for clarification.

'I am English, and Music trained, but chose Music as my teaching focus area, although I have had positions that combined both. My Australian school is flexible in what I teach.'

'Australia, I see.'

That left no room for anything more. Her tone suggested neither surprise, nor disdain.

'Howard will show you to your room, your students should arrive soon. You need to know that they come from a cross section of society, your butcher, baker, and candlestick maker types — you get the picture. Good to meet you.'

She turned and walked away without a departing hand-shake. Viola was relieved when she loped away. Her snobbery had no place in Viola Bardo's world, such an attitude was the breeding ground for prejudice. She hoped she would not have the misfortune to encounter Vanessa Smythe again! Cross-section of society! Was she not a part of the cross section? This assumed privilege was what divided society in the snobbery that the butcher and baker were undeserving of respect.

Howard entered, lifting her mood with his cheery, smiling face. He made her interview seem like a coffee hour with friends. His limited revelations about the college made her suspicious, but he was gracious in giving her the job.

'Hello there, good to see you again, Ms Bardo. Come along, your class arrives in ten minutes. How was it with Ms Smythe?'

Viola was sure his lower lip and eyebrow curled.

'It went well.'

'Good.'

She glanced at the roll.

'Ten students, is that all?'

'Yes, trust me that is ten too many!'

Here she was in a college and nobody cared about the students! How different from Aurora Academy where the student was a royal gift, but then again that depended on the power the parents wielded.

'Your password login and necessary resources are in the folder. Have a look through and let me know if you require more information? Have a pleasant first evening, Ms Bardo.'

He waltzed off, eager to get away when he saw her students arriving.

Viola's class of ten comprised eight men, balding and paunchy, with one young man built like a gym junkie. The two women ranged from twenty to fifty. The eldest had painted eyebrows arched in a permanent surprise. The other, less dramatic, sat at the back of the room.

Viola introduced herself, aware that she was facing a class of adults, most of whom were older than her. She dropped the Ms Bardo to Viola Bardo. A few deep breaths and nobody ventured forth to introduce themselves.

'Let us start from the back, left corner of the room, please introduce yourself.'

Nobody responded.

She pointed to the person in the left corner of the room. Perhaps she needed to simplify her use of English.

'Marquita. Sorry, my English is not good. Hello, nice to meet you.'

'Where are you from, Marquita?'

'Barcelona, but I live here six months now.'

'Good to meet you, Marquita.'

Viola looked at the next person. His eyes were glued to the floor. A voice from the right end of the room spoke up, the shiny-haired gym junkie with bulging arms on his desk.

'I'm Tony from Caracas. I am a painter but need to have this English certificate, the IELTS, to get an office job here.'

Viola was pleased that Tony was fluent in English and precise about who he was and why he was in her class. But he did not stop there.

'You are Viola Bardo. Are you a relative of Galleria Bardo?' He made the gallery seem like a person, she knew he meant her father.

'So, you know the gallery, yes I am a relative. Nice to meet you Tony.'

She looked in Marquita's direction to continue her introduction that Tony rudely interrupted. For someone who was a newcomer in the city, he was confident and clued up on the gallery.

Marquita said she failed the first test and had to pass this time. She added that her spoken English was acceptable, but her written skills needed work. The woman with the overarched eyebrows was silent, shaking her head.

Tony was loud and chatty again in wanting attention in between his male peers brief introductions.

'I have to pass this course, please give me extra work, Ms Viola.'

She was glad he dropped the question about her connection to the gallery. Media reports would be rife with the situation, and she had to avoid all questions. The two-hour lesson ended sooner than she expected.

Howard hovered at the door for her until the last student left. Tony called out over his shoulder.

'See you on Thursday Ms Viola, have a good night.'

'How was the session? Seems you have a fan already in Tony!'

'It went well, except this student,' she pointed to the roll, 'Modena said nothing at all.'

'Be careful with that one, she can be surly, it's best to leave her to her silent sulks. She's been here for two years, fails all the tests and returns each time.'

'Really? What does she do for a living?'

'She runs the pizza joint on the main street.'

'Is it necessary for her to have the certification of English proficiency?'

'No, she's a national so not sure what's going on there.'

'Interesting.'

'Anyway, I suspect this session has exhausted you. I have had a crazy day and I am eager to get home. Here are your keys to the classroom should you want to come in earlier on any evening. Nobody else is using this room. Please complete the remaining forms and submit them online. See you on Thursday like Tony says, but I won't stalk you,' he grinned and walked away.

His odd passing shot on Tony had her wondering why he found it necessary to make such a comment. Exchange positions brought a range of encounters, some good and some more weird than others. This one fell into the weird basket.

The air was cool outdoors. She buttoned up her jacket and walked home to blend with the locals. Two blocks down from the college, she spotted Modena talking to a young man and contemplated if he was her son. She appeared agitated, stepping backwards from him. Viola hurried away to avoid being noticed. It was a quiet night with a few couples, perhaps tourists, sitting in empty diners. Bustling city life was a safe distance away. She relished these quieter evenings before it was time to head back to Australia. With a toasted chicken and mayonnaise sandwich from the corner cafe, she quickened her pace to the apartment. A cup of tea and a look through Howard's folder was all she could manage before she called it a night.

Sebastian called as she settled down to watch the last news broadcast for the evening.

'Hello! How was your first night in class?'

'Hi Sebastian! It was good, but I suspect that is not the reason for your call.'

'That, and I wanted to know if you are going to work with Tempest on the matter at the gallery.'

'Yeah, I am, but my father will not be told about this. It is best to avoid him asking too many questions.'

'I agree. I might be getting ahead of myself here, but Tempest has asked me to assist you in whatever way I can. You know, look up people, investigate leads, etc. How do you feel about that?'

'Oh, that won't be necessary, the police being nudged by Tempest should work well, and besides no fresh incidents have occurred.'

'And still no news on the missing three. Just letting you know I am here. I should leave you to relax.'

'Thank you, I appreciate your offer of help. You don't have to rush off, I can chat for a wee while.'

She told him about her students and that she would have to adjust as much as they would in getting to know her.

'Any oddballs? Adults can present as fixed in their ways or have a few marbles missing.'

'It's too early for me to tell whether teenagers or adults are the same as students. I treat each with respect and care. They are a mixed batch, but that's the way it is.'

'Yeah, typical of life.'

She was finding her way around Sebastian. They were a

great duo on the Athens case. Her limited experience with men included a few work colleagues — no one she grew close to. Love affairs were not possible when she started her vigilante role. Anonymity was non-negotiable. Sebastian led an isolated life where his campus work was his only point of human contact. Her father lived with his head in the clouds most of the time. Self-reliance was a necessity, and she caught herself sometimes with her head in the clouds too, cut off from reality.

Once Sebastian said goodnight she was in the pit of self-despair, sad for her father, Sebastian, and the unseen Tempest who presented as a loner. Viola's mother was the only one walking on solid ground. She had her profession, a man, and dancing lessons that filled her non-teaching hours. On that note she picked up her journal.

> *Loneliness in a star-laden world*
> *happy and sad tonight*
> *waiting to see what comes with first*
>   *light*

With these hurried words in a faint scrawl, she fell asleep as her journal slid to the floor with a loud thump.

7

Viola wandered through the city, mesmerized by the multidimensional street murals. She had glimmers of artists' work in the city during her previous visits. Now every corner had a story to tell. She wished her father could be there, walking around with her to share this creative joy. The artworks that adorned the walls, from anamorphic to optical, and animals, drew her into the stories they told. The street art movement was a thriving, creative force, an unavoidable presence.

And yet three artists willingly or unwillingly disappeared from her father's gallery during a period of creative intensity. A magnetism she could not define, pulled her back to the street art in search of answers. Art and beauty combined had an opiate effect.

Somebody had to know something.

She was still a stranger in her father's birthplace, caught between the worlds of ancestry and choice.

Tourists lingered on street corners, awestruck by the visual extravaganza, and yet locals hurried about their daily business without a glance. Beauty had become commonplace. The human thirst for more, for difference, blinded the euphoria of discovering new meanings that art brought with each sighting. The artist's mood and emotions were gifted to the beholder.

Viola ambled to the waterway with her coffee, her head filled with thoughts on art — music, a canvas, or books with the capacity to invite changed perceptions across time. Would she feel the same ten years hence when she revisited the street murals that entranced her now?

Her mother extolled that permanence and perfection were the only way to live, but her university days gave her the freedom to refute this empty belief. The perfection imposed in her childhood, she now saw as superficial. For her perfection was in the imperfections — life's challenges unleashed the best in people. Her father was a classic example. When his marriage to her mother crumbled, he produced art drawn from his deep well of fractured emotions, hidden beneath a jocular veneer. His international recognition came when he was grieving for Lorenza, and it was in that period that he returned to his ancestral home. Was pain necessary as the seat of creative brilliance, or life's struggles the engineer of greatness? What challenges did the street artists suffer to bring the city to life with their pulsating imaginations. Ah! The cruelty, or beauty of life? For beauty to be born, it was imperative to channel pain. Then truth and beauty harmonized. The eye of the soul opened without inhibition in strife. Viola questioned whether the rational mind ceased to exist during creative brilliance.

She absorbed both, on her journey, to find a balance for the best between them.

* * *

SHE STROLLED to the mural in the secluded lane she discovered on her first walkabout. The stranger, in a state of deshabille, as he was when she last saw him, stared at a mural, transfixed as though he had never left. The mural that captivated him, today, was on the opposite wall to the previous one that held his attention. This mural also had an image of a child, a boy, with black spiky hair. She stood aside to leave him to his private moment.

He sensed her behind him.

'You are back. Why?'

Viola paused, unsure if the question was directed at her or whether he was talking to himself.

'As you are back,' she answered in a loud voice.

This bold retaliation was the only way to conceal her mounting fear from being detected — her learned way to steel herself. She had her mother to thank for that lesson.

Let no one, more especially a man, know your weakness, your fear, your breaking point. Then you have lost the battle to a free you.

The stranger's reply sent a quivering bolt through her limbs.

'Yes, I am. I have a reason. You don't!'

He walked away in his unsteady gait, and brushed past her, his eyes lowered.

His unwashed body odor lingered.

She did not turn around to watch him leave. His ankle length striped coat swished against her bare calf. It was stiff with age and dirt. He might be an iconic street person in these parts, but it would be pointless asking her father if he knew the stranger. Placido rarely came into the city. The wayfarer fascinated her with his mysterious air.

She had the urgency to scribble down her thoughts on him.

Words tumbled out onto her phone. The dank smell of burned wood clung to the air in the narrow lane.

> *Wayfarer who are you?*
> *A human figure from the wall*
> *in your striped tattered coat*
> *a ghostly presence—archaic*
> *perhaps from another realm*
> *Will we meet again?*

That afternoon she decided to speak to her father to gauge his thoughts on the culture on the streets. The stranger appeared homeless. Surely, he would know something about the underworld here.

'Papa, how are you? Have you had word from Martens Direito whether I can return to the gallery soon, or have greater levity granted on my visitation? Sorry, papa, that, makes it sound like you are in prison!'

'It feels that way knowing that you are close, and I can't get to you. Martens thinks we need to hang on for a few more days. I don't want to push too many buttons. It might seem selfish of me in the eyes of the artists loyally standing by me, if I jeopardize the investigation by expecting preferential treatment.'

'Yes, I agree, I apologize for expecting that. One visit, a week would make me happy.'

'I understand. Our patience shall be rewarded.'

Placido's positivity and calmness surprised her. She wanted to ask if he was on the grog again and knew it was better to curb her tongue. It was not the right moment to tell him about the stranger. He would be distressed if he felt she was in danger.

'How are the artists coping with this partial incarceration?'

'Hardly that, Artista. Now they are in the throes of their creative work, so it blocks all else out during those hours. We are keeping it as normal as we can around here to avoid further rumblings.'

'Good! Do not allow this impasse to mar your creativity. Sometimes artists are at the mercy of those who criticize their work and passion.'

'Tell me about it! Your mother was my pervasive critic, but I agree, the police could be of that mind. Hence, I am prohibited from leaving the gallery. How is teaching going? Why are you not working tonight, meu filho?'

'My classes are on Tuesday and Thursday nights, and if the college requires me for another evening, it might be Fridays.'

Viola slipped into a childlike tone when her father was tender.

'Please, if you do not mind me asking, why do you need to work while you are on holiday?'

'I need to keep busy, papa, under the current climate, or my mind will kill me. I can withstand anything if it does not involve my personal life... you... my papa... I worry.'

Viola swallowed her threatening tears. She missed her disorganized father who would, on a whim, make her caramel popcorn to soothe her fears. Now her strength for him was summoned.

'Ah! Like father, like child! No tears now, Artista!'

She heard the smile in his voice and knew he was trying his best to cope to keep her from worrying.

The stranger was insignificant in her papa's aura. She saved that conversation for another day. He was in good spirits and that canceled her fears. The stranger's face remained in the familiarity of his eyes. A ragged beard concealed the greater part of his face, but his sad, bright, black eyes harked to something in her memory. Something she could not recall.

Viola spent the rest of the day researching street art in the country. The detailed information available on the internet gave her a wealth of understanding on the artists' backgrounds and works. After three hours, she was thirsty and peckish. Her head did a swoop that unsteadied her when she stood up. She hung onto the desk for a moment until it passed. A chilled glass of water refreshed her muzzy head. Perhaps she needed reading glasses or was it the frequent consumption of fast food that messed with her body. She touched her belly and scowled at its protrusion. Weight had piled on from her many trips to the ice-cream parlor before Sebastian left for America. The memory of pistachio ice-cream made her salivate. Her mother would no doubt comment on her thickening girth! Thankfully, it would be a few months before she saw her again. Now she gave a toss about her mother's opinions. The damage was deep, but maturity had a way of shoving the non-essentials of life out the window. She would watch her health, not her weight. Having a svelte silhouette was no longer a priority. A morning jog three times a week might do her a world of good. Health first, so two boiled eggs it was for an early dinner with a bit of wilted baby spinach and a strong cup of coffee. The decadent croissants from the corner patisserie faded from memory.

Her dizzy spells were frequent since her arrival, and she had to take control of her wellness if she hoped to get to the bottom of Galleria Bardo's mystery.

Viola rose before the birds, donned her active wear, which she dragged out from the bottom of her bag. It sat there ever since she left Greece. She hit the streets in her well-worn sneakers that trod many miles in her investigative duties in Athens. The only luxury she allowed herself on Tempest's missions was a pair of comfortable pumps and sneakers. If she could wear her sneakers in the classroom she would, but most schools expected a level of professional dress. She ached for her laid-back lifestyle in Australia. Home shores, the familiar and predictable, made life a breeze. Yet, while there she craved the adrenalin of a new investigation, the danger, the unfolding of truths and the hopeful sweet resolution. She was away from home for almost half of any year in the last three years. Money was always tight with the casual or contract work she took on while working on a case. Teaching gave her the flexibility to fulfill both passions. Her shoestring budget forced her to take on work at the English night school. The vacation she expected was not under her command.

She was breathless when the inhospitable pre-dawn chill

hit her face. Slate gray fog hung low over the city, making the horizon a bleak fusion of muted tones caught inside a twirling mist. Cobbled streets added character to the city, but she had to be vigilant to avoid injury by not tripping on the stones. The fog surrounded her, making her feet invisible. A slow jog was safest with poor visibility. It was the first morning she ventured out this early. The empty cafes seemed to whisper as she passed windowed shop fronts. A ghost town in winter and over-populated in summer. It was two weeks away from Christmas. The streets were pretty this time of year. She recalled spending Christmas during a holiday to Lisbon with her father — the smell of chestnuts in the air, glimmering lights by night, and shimmering tinsel by day, warmed the celebratory mood.

Her love for Portuguese cuisine came from her father, who ensured she imbibed that part of her heritage and culture. She straddled four cultures and deserved a seat at the table of the United Nations! African, French, Portuguese and Australian! Easing her way from country to country, she blended into the cultures she encountered, although human behavior of some, did not rise to the richness of their respective cultures.

Sunrise struggled on the horizon, but cloud cover was set to stay, stubborn in allowing warm days to come through. A forty-minute jog was her plan to feel energized to face the day. She switched to a brisk walk when the thin, crisp air challenged her breathing. Her buttoned jacket and zippered hood which kept her hair in place did nothing to prevent the chill from biting through. When her coffee craving hit, she hurried back to her apartment. Cafes opened around nine. As the fog lifted, she balked at the rancid stench of food from laden bins outside cafes and restaurants. It was a relief to be back at the apartment where everything was fresh and still with tenants blissfully asleep.

Today was her stay at home day.

After a lengthy, indulgent shower, she pulled on a loose jumper that she tossed into her bag from the cupboard at the gallery, and crawled into bed with a large mug of coffee. It was good to feel clear-headed and invigorated, but the snug bedcovers held sweet comfort as she dozed off, enveloped in its warmth.

Around 8 am Placido called, apologetic that he disturbed her beauty sleep. He knew she loved her sleep-ins during her school breaks, and Helena forbid it as irresponsible and lazy.

'Out jogging on an icy, wet morning, Artista? And it was foggy.'

'I enjoyed it, and besides when it's cold you don't notice the rain. I had the city to myself!'

'You might well have. People do not rise early here in winter or on rainy days during the holiday season, except you!'

She heard the wheeze in his chuckle.

'So why are you up this early, papa?'

'I'm cooking a pot of tripe and white beans this morning to warm up the household, except you're not here!'

'I wish I could be there to help you!'

'Anyway, I am sorry to tell you I don't have good news from Martens.'

'Why? What is it?' Her throat tightened and her relaxed muscles stiffened.

'Police have instructed him to inform you not to leave Porto for the next thirty days. Lord have mercy! I'm so sorry about this mess.'

'It's not your fault, but I wonder what is going on behind the scenes. We are told nothing! Just more restrictions imposed.'

'I had a surprise trip to Lisbon booked for us. Remember that Christmas we spent there?'

'I do and thought about it when I was out this morning. Tell

Martens to appeal this restriction, that you have a booking from a while ago.'

'It will make no difference. Trust me. I will mention it to him but would not count on anything going in our favor. They have also put a restriction on my artists — they can't leave, and I am cooking until Madalena is allowed to return.'

'It gets messier each day. The saving-grace is that the situation has halted with no one else disappearing. Can I at least spend Christmas with you?'

'Oh, how could I forget to tell you something so important? You have permission to spend Christmas Day with me. I am not sure if you are allowed to stay over. Madalena may be allowed to return on Christmas Eve for the preparations. At least we have that.'

'When you are a beggar, any crumb is a banquet.'

'We are viewed as having a hand in this mess, but I am happy that you will be with me for Christmas.'

'Papa, is that tripe still cooking, or are you finished with the preparation? I want to talk to you for a while longer and do not want your meal burning while I rattle on.'

'In the middle of cooking, meu filho, I'll call you back if you are going to be staying in today.'

She wanted to tell her papa she was having dizzy spells but held back. The familiar stranger took precedence.

Viola worked on her lesson preparation and looked through the IELTS requirements. Her night class was a mixed bag. Some registered for English, but others were doing the IELTS which offered international opportunities especially for people working across countries. Others did the Preliminary Cambridge English course. English proficiency was held in high esteem — it opened more doors as it did for migrants in Australia.

English and music kept her soul in motion — music filtered

into all aspects of her life — she had her literary mother and artist father to thank for that. Her album on her piano ensemble was making its debut around the world, although few knew about it. The principal at Aurora College somehow knew about her album. It was under the cover name, *Loren Soul,* to honor her aunt. Her poetry pen name was *Artista B.* If all went to plan, her poetry collection would hit the retail world next Christmas. She had plans, so many plans, but when the winds of justice called, she had to change direction.

Viola felt a psychic connection to Tempest, who always called on cue when she needed support. No listening devices, just that across the soul waves connection that lit up her cell phone screen.

'Tempest! You literally jumped out of my thoughts!' she laughed.

'Wonderful to hear the joy in your voice. Dare I assume that you have good news?'

Viola sighed after a long pause.

'Oh, I wish I did. Papa is positive, so that helps as does hearing your voice.'

'Give me some insight into your papa, the man, the father, the artist. Then, I will fill you in on my plan.'

Viola knew that Tempest was indulging her, trying to ease her concerns.

'I will need a month to fill you in on Placido Bardo! He is a complex man, but I would not have him any other way. He is eccentric, a messy artist who produces the finest work. But he is kind and sensitive. His problem is he wears his heart on his sleeve. Over the years, wannabe artists exploited him. He squandered money on every artist who came to him with a sob story. Once they got what they wanted, they disappeared, and papa was never one to put up a fight. In the divorce from my mother, he let her do as she wanted. Her happiness is all he cared about. His crushing blow came when his sister disappeared, but his solace was Galleria Bardo, his mausoleum to her memory. She would be so proud of all that he has achieved. Having no closure has aged him, he has become neglectful of his health. Oh, and he loves cooking! I spoke to him before your call and he was cooking tripe and white beans for the artists in residence.'

Tempest listened and only interjected when she heard food mentioned.

'What was he cooking?'

'Tripe, and white beans.'

Viola assumed she had to explain the finer elements of Portuguese cuisine.

'Offals. Tripe is the belly of the...'

'I know what tripe is. I know it is a delicacy. But perhaps not the best for your father if his health needs attention.'

The wonderful Tempest was quick to react to Viola's concern for Placido. Her care and compassion made her an ideal leader.

'Yes, not good at all for him, but I did not have the heart to tell him. The police have denied me permission to stay with him, so I cannot check on what he consumes. This time of year, brings out the worst eating habits in people.'

Viola felt the stinging guilt of her peanut brittle addiction.

Tempest heard her defensiveness of her father's poor eating habits, and silently applauded their father daughter love. She let the moment pass and swung back to business in her usual way.

'I have some information from a source I consulted. There is a crime organization operating within the territory emanating from a worldwide crime ring. They exploit artists for money. The precise nature of this underbelly is unknown, but we have a starting point.'

'Papa is wiser now so I don't think he will allow exploitation, especially from a crime base.'

'I understand, but you need to be open to how this could be a possibility at the gallery with your father being innocent of this exploitation. It might be through the very team inside the gallery in his residence program.'

How could Tempest make such an assumption when she had not met the artists her father had approved to attend his workshops? Beautiful people who were supporting him. She had to keep a check on her emotions when anger surfaced on whether this could be possible.

Tempest picked up Viola's unease.

'Remember, it is only something we need to consider. You should be observant during your days at the gallery and interact as much as possible with the visiting artists.'

'How will I do that when I'm only allowed to visit for Christmas Day?'

'Somehow you need to ask your father, without raising his suspicion, to do a bit of sleuthing. You will find a way.'

Viola pondered upon the gravitas of Tempest's words after she wafted off.

9

Mural Man, her private dubbing of the stranger, left Viola in a quandary, compelled to find out who he was, and why he seemed attached to the laneway murals.

It was Thursday evening and a walk to the college added to her commitment to keep up a regular exercise schedule. The rhythm would clear her head and keep her body active. Working two days a week created a sedentary working lifestyle, researching and preparing lessons in an area that was not her passion. Exercise lessened her dizzy spells. She kept an eating diary and a close eye on when the dizziness occurred. After doctor Horatio's dental work in Athens, she was not ready to see a doctor here.

Leaving home earlier, gaining an extra half hour, helped her extend her step count with another brisk walk around the building before class. She missed the evening news on these nights. Tony was the first student to arrive, armed with questions on Galleria Bardo.

'Good evening, Miss Viola, have you seen the news tonight?'

'No, sorry Tony, I came in early to set up my powerpoint…'

She dared not ask him what he saw on the news. Her curiosity or rather his perceived sense of her curiosity would open a door she did not want to enter with him.

'Galleria Bardo was on the news, terrible business, three artists — *three* missing, and nobody knows where they are.'

Viola had to be careful how she responded to him. Her father's protection was her prerogative.

'I will try to watch a replay of the news later. That does not sound good, but I am sure there will be answers soon. I have some work to finish up, why don't you take a seat and do some reading or go over our previous work.'

'That's okay, I'll sit here and wait for the others.'

Viola cringed, she needed time to compose herself. Her father had not indicated that the media was reporting the matter. She was a Bardo and everyone who knew she was would ask about her association with the gallery. Tony was a curious young man who enjoyed a chat. She had to appear detached from what was going on in her father's life while she was at the college.

She could leave nothing open for student speculation. Tony seemed harmless enough. A bit too much gel in his curly locks, but harmless. He plonked himself on the desktop in front of her teacher table, her ears burned, and she opted to turn to the computer screen away from his gaze. Tony watched her with arms folded in boredom, wanting to talk. Soon the next student sauntered in, greeted her, and took his seat. Tony swooped in and perched himself on the desktop next to him. Students sitting on their desks always irritated Viola. Tonight, she chose not to say anything to Tony to give him leeway to suspect her unease. She heard him ask the student if he had watched the six o'clock news. His eyes penetrated the back of her head as he asked the question. Her back tightened, trying to preserve her equanimity. She was good at composing herself under stressful situations, but this time it took every ounce of her energy. Tony dragged it out as each of the nine students arrived. All thankfully had not watched the early evening news, so the conversation shut down.

Tonight's two-hour lesson dragged for an eternity. When it was over, she saw Howard waiting at her door.

Tony walked towards her, saw Howard, lingered for a second and left. Viola hoped he had made his trek home and was not loitering in the corridor, waiting for her. He was bent on probing what she had to say about the business at Galleria Bardo.

Howard handed her another folder, and watched Tony walk away.

'The IELTS' requirements I told you about. Are you finding Tony a bit of a nuisance? Let me know. I could have a word with him. He can be persistent, at times.'

Viola wanted to ask whether there were previous situations where Tony proved to be a nuisance. Her fragile nerves could not accommodate such a conversation with Howard. What was it with prying men tonight?

Howard continued uninvited.

'Tony Braganza is quite a charmer. I recommend you keep your distance. He is a clinger. You know what I mean. Soon he will follow you home. He likes a pretty face.'

Viola annoyance flared. How dare Howard insinuate she was a brainless pretty face, or that she was unaware of how to conduct herself? She spoke like one floating, watching herself say something she hoped would not ruin her position at the college.

'Thank you for your advice and the folder. I am on my way out now. You have a pleasant evening.'

Howard's smirk was more irritating than his insinuation. She thought he was the better administrator. What was it that he was not saying? Two days a week, she could do it! Nobody was going to ruffle her feathers. She preferred to have a frank conversation on perhaps Tony's history. If there was one, she needed to be alerted. No subtle hints dropped. Oh, the frustration of Howard's male superiority! Her intuition which served her well would guide her to the truth he was hiding. She liked him when they met, thought he was open and honest like Rob Dwyer, but it seemed she was mistaken. Then again, Sebastian left her dubious after their first meeting until she got to know him. She let this irritation with Howard pass. It was trivial in light of everything in her path.

Viola saw Vanessa Smythe in the hallway, and pulled her head back in. The last thing she needed this evening was a stilted conversation, if she could call it a conversation, with Ms Smythe. Nothing was worth the risk of being accosted by the campus head.

The air outside refreshed her. She pulled her hood over her head, snuggled her hands into her pockets and made a note to carry gloves on Tuesday evening. Close to the second block from the college, she saw a shapeless coat gliding down a dim lane. Mural Man! She drew back into the shadow of a dark doorway and waited a few seconds. Tonight, she would follow him. His uncanny presence, wherever she was, gave Tempest's speculations a ring of possibility. He was following her! People hunkered down at home tonight. A smattering of hurrying folk paid no attention to her silhouette in the doorway of the shut dry cleaners.

One casual stroller behind Mural Man offered her obscurity as she followed from a safe distance. She had to ensure she was far enough — he had a heightened sense whenever she was close, or perhaps when anybody was near him. He hobbled along with a pronounced drag of his left foot. His energized bounce conveyed his urgency.

Viola dived into another doorway when the figure in front of her veered to the left. Now she had to skulk along the walls of buildings to avoid detection. Mural Man walked to the furthest end of the city and abruptly stopped in front of a rundown warehouse. The creaking roller door opened magically when he approached, as though accessed by remote control. Common sense told her there was no electricity in this derelict building. Mural Man bent and entered the dark building. She watched as the rusty doors rolled down and clanged with hostile finality.

Viola traced her steps back to the second block from the college to find her way home. It was well after 11 pm when she arrived at the apartment. She drew a map of where the warehouse was located. What was it? Why was he in there? It was a freezing night, and with no electricity, the place would be uninhabitable. She recalled the odor of charred wood rising from his striped coat.

This might be his dwelling place.

Another night of lost sleep as she researched warehouses only to find scores lay vacant. So many buildings, with broken, once picturesque, blue, and white mosaic tiles that might have been grand and bustling in their day — now ghostly shadows housing a past that nobody seemed keen to rekindle? Relics without a history. Some wine cellars in their heyday. Yet the city had an allure she could not define. And inside a crumbling warehouse was Mural Man — somebody had to have opened the door for him from inside. Did he have a family housed there? Her father would refer to Mural Man's unkempt appearance as his *desgrenhado* state.

This stranger had her attention, and she had to know more about him. He seemed to be part of this city's underbelly. One she was keen to unveil.

* * *

IT WAS time to enlist Sebastian's help. It was almost 7 pm in New York when Sebastian picked up her call.

'Hey Viola! Up late tonight! Everything OK?'

'Hi Sebastian, it depends on what you mean by, 'OK.' I hope I have not interrupted you at this hour.'

'I'm still at my desk at work. Teaching is over for the day, but I am swamped with marking and am loath to cook a meal tonight so I ordered a pizza which should be here in half an hour. Security will not allow the delivery man into the building, so I must trek all the way out to pick it up! Talk to me about what's happening there.'

'I'm really sorry to disturb your marking, I had a strange experience tonight after class. I wandered out of the city almost and saw many abandoned buildings. I know you are going to ask why I was walking around at night. I have a good reason.'

'Be careful, Viola. Cities are sinister at night, and you should not be wandering off to isolated parts. You know the stories we hear about tourists who do this in places they are not familiar with.'

'I'm really not a tourist, you know. I look like a local returning home from work.'

'This late? I still say watch your back. There is no rhyme or reason why the artists are missing from the gallery. Avoid abandoned parts of the city.'

It was time to tell Sebastian about Mural Man.

He listened in silence.

'You are being baited. How could you not know you are

being followed? This Mural Man led you to that warehouse. Why else would be appear a block away from the college on the night you're teaching?'

A shiver ran through her.

'You tell me, Sebastian. If you see this stranger, you might have a different opinion. He seems a homeless person.'

'My gut tells me he knows more about you than you do about him.'

'Are you suggesting his connection to Galleria Bardo's issues? What if he is just an innocent street person?'

'Innocent street person? Are they ever?'

'That is cold and unfair. Why are you skeptical about this stranger? I want plausible reasons without preconceived judgements.'

'He has an interest in murals or one particular piece of street art, right? Your father is a renowned artist and runs a gallery that was once the pinnacle of the creative world.'

'I still don't get where you are driving this? There is some-thing about Mural Man's eyes, I can't quite put my finger on why there is an air of familiarity about him.'

'Surely that suggests why he might stalk you? He wants something from you. Perhaps he knows your father?'

'My father, Placido? How would he know anybody like Mural Man?'

'May I, with your permission, off course, investigate the situation from here, using what you have told me. I know I can snoop around the underbelly there to get a sense of what might have happened to the three missing artists.'

'That would be great if you could. I will let Tempest know about the latest developments.'

'Thank you for trusting me. I will do everyone I can to lift the lid on this. You said there was a student in your class tapping you about your connection to the gallery. Do you think he might know something?'

'Tony? No way! He is just a curious young man. I cannot imagine him knowing Mural Man.'

Sebastian knew Viola never prejudged people and detested defining individuals by external appearances. It was hard, cold facts only, for her, not speculations and denigration.

'How would you describe this Mural Man, the person you perceive, not his physical appearance?'

'I think he is a lost soul, harboring pain, and finds meaning or solace in the murals. He seems to have claimed ownership over them because my presence irritated him.'

'Would you be able to send me a photograph or video of the two murals?'

'I could do so tomorrow, and hopefully he won't be there before me.'

'But please be careful.'

'I am always careful and besides I'm here to help my father, so my safety is essential.'

'Glad to hear that.'

Sebastian's older voice was not the younger brother she perceived when they met in Athens.

'I have to hurry. Jasper would have chewed up the couch by now!'

'Jasper? The puppy?'

'Yeah, it's great to have a welcoming, wagging tale when I get home.'

'I am so happy to hear that he is a great companion. He is one lucky puppy to have you as an owner.'

'Thank you. You have had an eventful night so off to bed with you! And dare I say it, no peanut brittle for you, young lady!'

. . .

Viola rolled into the bed covers, happy that Sebastian was going to do his bit from New York to make sense of the pieces to a mystery that caught her off-guard. A morning jog, a sneaked in video or photograph of the murals, two blocks down from her apartment, was her plan for the morning.

10

Dreams and memories arrive without warning to an unsettled mind. The familiarity of Mural Man puzzled Viola. His haunting eyes, and wobbling gait troubled her. Who was he, played over and over?

* * *

SHE WAS a child running down the streets of Porto as she did today. Her father walked ahead of her, turning now and then to tease her to hurry. Everything she saw moved in slow rolling motion. Arms lifted and fell with robotic ease, legs long and languid, seemed to take an eternity to drop from mid-air to her side. Urgency took hold. She had to catch up with her father.

Then, as if a switch had turned off — the sunny day turned indigo, then black.

Her father gone!

Viola called out in a fearful croaking voice, her heart thumping.

'Papa! Papa! I can't see you! Papa, where are you!'

She tripped on the cobbled street. Picked herself up and looked behind, looked ahead, undecided whether to advance or retrace her steps. A familiar voice sent a chill tingling through her limbs.

'You again? Why are you always here?'

Mural Man stood in front of her.

Looming, gigantic, and overpowering.

Her voice deserted her. Tears welled into rivulets.

She was alone.

Her father was nowhere in sight.

Mural Man was here, so close, and nobody else was on the dark street. He reached out to lift her. Her voice cracked in a blood-curdling scream. It echoed down the street and bounced back to her.

Viola jumped bolt upright in her bed, drenched in a cold sweat, panting like she had run a long distance. Blinking to clear the memory, she shivered as the morning air penetrated through the covers. She wriggled, unsure of her whereabouts, lowered herself in the bed until her chin was safely covered. She lay there for an hour.

Was Mural Man a threat to her and her father? What did he want?

She crawled out of bed, still not sure where she was. The curtain rolled and unfurled. She hurried to shut the window, sure that she had shut the window last night, then recalled that she was in the apartment. Coffee was a necessity to settle her frazzled nerves and jolt her waning energy.

This morning was not good for a jog.

It was time to call Tempest again. She needed clarity. Her dream had left her vulnerable, wanting guidance on how to proceed. Aunt Lorenza said dreams came as messages of caution, and it was up to her how she interpreted and acted on them. She emphasized that they should not be ignored.

Another shiver ripped through her with that thought. It was not her dream alone; her beloved papa was a significant part of it. The similarity of this dream to the night before her aunt disappeared unnerved her. Was her father in danger, or was she? Could it be possible that her dream foreshadowed that she was the threat to Galleria Bardo? *They*, whoever they were, took the first artist the night before she arrived from Athens. Argh! Questions poked like a knife thrower's misaligned pointy end. Answers were urgent, and she had to stop her dalliance. Her emotional connection to the case altered her behavior and needed conscious correcting.

All she could hold down was a mug of black coffee as waves of nausea came and went. With no direct telephonic contact, she relied on her email being opened by Tempest. Martens had to arrange for her to have more days at the gallery. Her father needed to be watched and cautioned. His absentmindedness increased with distress. As much as he put on a chirpy disposition, she knew it was to keep her from worrying. He shielded her from all the trials and tribulations of girlhood, always at loggerheads with Helena's hard-line parenting.

Memory flooded back on all the times her father challenged the misjudgements of her character as early as her first year at school. With his faith in her, she pursued a teaching career with a commitment to justice for the voiceless.

She was all the daughters to her beloved father who never failed to eradicate her fears.

* * *

Tempest called an hour after she received Viola's email.

'Viola, how are you and your dear papa? Any news?'

'Thank you for your swift call. No news, sorry to say. But

something is bothering me, which I think is linked to the case at the gallery.'

Tempest took in everything Viola reported on Mural Man, remained silent after the recount, and then spoke.

'Your dream is not your subconscious. It is what is happening in the now. Fear manifests in varying ways as it seeks an outlet. The hooks to your childhood and Mural Man have your papa as the common denominator. You have correctly linked this stranger with your papa. Fear of losing a parent or any loved one is a scar that recurs through our psyche when we are challenged. This wayfarer is connected to you and your papa. Your sixth sense has pointed you to the familiar in this person you call Mural Man. Keep your journal going and I will conduct research from my end, but if you can find out the legal identity of this stranger, this will speed up things from my end. You are being warned to proceed with caution. Your hypersensitivity is peaked so note everything. Dreams are reflections of your waking self and might persist until resolved. Try to hold back the visions during your daily activities to keep a clear head for what you need to observe. I have not suggested this to you before.'

Tempest paused, coughed, and waited for Viola to react. She was silent, waiting to hear what was being suggested.

'Practice the art of meditation every morning to clear your way for the day ahead. If you cannot do this on your own, I will send you a video on how to start. Soon it will become second nature. But it's imperative that you begin as soon as possible.'

'I can do that. I need to steer my thoughts now because I am emotionally hooked to the situation. Vince, the American teacher at Aurora Academy spoke of the benefits of meditation.'

'Good! All will unfold as the universe desires. Trust that. Now, are you ready for positive news?'

Viola waited, barely able to breathe.

'I negotiated with the police to allow you more days at the gallery.'

'Really? Thank you so much! Papa will be happy.'

'Don't you want to know how many days?'

'Yes, yes, please!'

'Four days a week that could be the weekend and two weekdays. Generous, I think after complete prohibition. You must inform Martens twenty-four hours before you arrive. On no account should you approach the police directly. That will blow it!'

'I am grateful for what you have achieved for me to be with papa and will a hundred percent adhere to the rules.'

Viola knew that Tempest's concern was that her emotions might trigger erratic reactions. She was feeling her way around Viola in this family matter.

'While you are at the gallery for the extra days, use the time wisely to question the artists still in residence. Get inside their heads. I know I can count on you to do this. Someone knows something. I'll be in touch.'

Tempest was gone.

11

'Four days together, Artista! I knew the stars would align to get you back home as we hoped! Although I should say thanks to Martens.'

Placido was a boy again with a rosy hue in his round cheeks and an infectious cackle.

'I know nothing can ever keep us apart, papa, even from across the ocean, I always hang onto that!' Viola tugged at her father's longer than usual neglected beard. Tempest exerted her influence to bring them together but Viola let her father believe that Martens and the stars conspired in their favor.

'Please thank Martens for me when you next speak. I am here for two successive days. Shall we plan dinner for the artists? My homecoming dinner!'

She laughed, absorbing her father's joyous energy.

'That sounds wonderful. I will check in with the team to see if they are up to it. All are in the euphoric state of new creations, so socializing is not always an option, but I will ask.'

'You do that, papa, and I'll tidy up the place. Will

Madalena return soon? She's a far better cook than the both of us, we must admit!'

'I will not push any favors with the police and risk losing this time with you. My cooking has improved, it will please you to know.'

Soon the kitchen in this quiet, shut gallery was abuzz with clanging pots and pans, bubbling and sizzling sounds. Placido used every pot and dish in the kitchen. The sink was Monte Binga with precarious piles of dishes in every size and shape.

Tidiness was second nature to Viola. A messy space made her anxious. Thanks to her pedant mother, everything in her clothing cupboard was color coded and itemized according to the seasons and Helena's moods.

Christmas was clinical in her childhood home before her parent's divorce. When Lorenza visited in the good old days, she brought laughter and music with her. After a few glasses of wine, she strummed her guitar and sang out of tune. Then silence followed in the ear-shattering absence of conversation when dark clouds haloed her mother's head. The harsh clanging of tidying up halted the merriment.

Today Viola and Placido cooked to the tune of soft jazz in the background as he waltzed from the stove to the fridge and sink with the rhythmic swaying of his arms. He was aglow that his Artista was with him — a blissful time in the imperfections of their lives.

Dinner with the artists who were grateful to share a meal with the Bardo's lifted the community spirit at the gallery. They spent the first hour savoring the delectable meal and chatting about flavors and ingredients that Placido favored. Viola waited for the right moment to gauge their interest in street art. After a cheese, crackers, carrot cake and coffee dessert, she asked for the artists thoughts on local street murals.

Crystal replied but her brother, Dillon, threw her a

concerned look. She had visited the city a few times and enjoyed losing herself in the laneways of vibrant, soulful art.

Viola snatched this moment to probe whether Crystal had a special wall.

'It is really difficult to narrow it down to just one wall. All are quite unique in some way. Superb! If I have to give an answer, it would be the child releasing a dove.'

'What about it captivates you?'

'I think the symbol of freedom and purity against the dilapidated buildings in the background. It's hopeful for the next generation.'

'Beautiful thoughts, I must make a point of finding it.'

'We seek connections in art, so this mural reminds me of my family's practice of releasing white doves at midnight on New Year's Eve as a symbol of heading into the future.'

'What a wonderful poetic gesture! You must come from a large family. I can almost see the doves against the sky! That is a special memory.'

Viola turned to look at the artist who responded to Crystal.

I think I have favorite — the wall with the forlorn child peering into the distance from behind a large rock that conceals his slight frame. The symbolism and sadness in that wall grabs me every time I see it.'

Viola listened, eager to know if it was the same painting that transfixed Mural Man. Before she could probe further, Dillon shared his special find among the city's street art. The mural with the young man in a baseball cap with his arms folded, fascinated him in exuding fear and defiance.

She photographed Mural Man's favorite paintings because of her unexplained connection to them. The desire to pass it around the group excited her, but had to be quelled. Placido remarked that art anywhere was a masterpiece when it moved the viewer.

'Yes, papa, I agree, it's like reading poetry or a delightful book. You feel the nucleus, the pulse of the piece, yet each one of us views it with a unique, curious eye.'

The conversation flowed and each had a say except one. Alonso had a vacant stare, he was physically present but mentally disconnected.

Soon all headed to their cottages saying they had overindulged in the delicious meal and extended their gratitude for the evening. Alonso was the first one out the door.

'Thank you, Artista for suggesting this get together. Everybody enjoyed the evening.'

'You think so, papa? Alonso was quiet throughout dinner, and seemed to shut off during our discussion on street art.'

'He is the silent type in the group on the whole, so it was not unusual to see him this way. I admit he seems broodier this week. The creative stage in his work makes him unapproachable. His paintings are dark and gloomy to match his personality. Nothing to worry about.'

'I get that but not to make an attempt to engage when your host invited you to a special dinner? That is plain rude in my book.'

'Not everyone you meet will have your impeccable manners.'

'I'm not judging him at all. I find him strange. Dillon is quiet but engages when he has something of worth to contribute. I might try to chat with Alonso tomorrow, if he allows me in. I feel the pressure to know what is on his mind. It sure is weighing him down. He looked more troubled than preoccupied.'

'The teacher in you is more aware of human body language than I am. I know you are always gentle but try not to rattle him. The last thing I want is another artist disappearing on me.'

'I will be cautious, papa, I promise.'

The buzz of the evening brought a longing to have Lorenza back. Tonight, she would have offered advice on how to proceed with Alonso, or she might have coerced a word or two out of him. She had the ability to draw people into her space. Viola needed to feel her radiance.

'Papa, let's take a walk to the gallery.'

'You want to talk to Lorenza? You did that for a long time after she left. I would hear you at night in a conversation and then hear your sobs. I believe she is in heaven, meu filho, looking down on us, watching over us.'

'I wish I knew that for sure, that she is at rest, no longer roaming the earth.'

The words 'died' or 'passed on' never entered Viola's head when she spoke of her aunt. Hope lived with her as much as it did with her father.

Placido turned on a spotlight above the life size painting of his beloved sister. Her deep eyes under blue shaded eyelids had a teasing glint. Gold streaks of light caught the edges of the canvas and reflected on the floor around Viola's feet.

'That is amazing, she is with us, I feel it, papa.'

They stared up at her image. The woman who brought so much love and joy to their lives.

'You know the best are taken from us, too soon, to serve a higher purpose.'

Viola made no response. She refused to acknowledge the finality of her father's words. In that moment he seemed to have resolved his grief.

'Papa, did aunt Lorenza have many male admirers?'

'She sure did, men and women were drawn to her warmth and charm.'

'But was there someone special? A lover perhaps?'

'She never spoke of that side of her life, no dates, no young men called. Not any that I know. You are so much like Lorenza in your need for solitude.'

'Just like you do!'

Viola squeezed her father's arm.

'Yes, I blame myself that the investigation became a cold case. I was too grief-stricken to question and pursue the matter. I regret that to this day. Not knowing is worse than knowing. One never rests.'

Placido was good at masking his feelings in the outside world, but with Viola he was vulnerable and raw.

'I was too young to understand what happened back then. Do you have copies of the reports and the names of the detectives involved?'

'I do have them in a safe deposit box in Mozambique. Why do you ask, Artista?'

'I want to know more.'

'Don't dig up old bones, it will cause more pain.'

'I won't papa. You were many years older than her.'

'Yes, sometimes I felt more like her father than her older brother. As she went missing, our father never returned from work one day, and a month later his remains turned up in Johannesburg. How he got there remains a mystery to this day.'

'Appears as though fate commands ill-begotten disappearances in our family.'

'Sadness surrounded my sister's life. My mother died having her, and my father was never the same after that. That might have contributed to his mysterious disappearance. But who knows? I vowed I would never leave you floundering after the divorce. I fought to keep the marriage, but your mother wanted out and she had her way.'

'You were always too soft, papa. I recall hearing aunt Lorenza scolding you for not having grit in your blood.'

They both had a hearty laugh.

'Lorenza was tough on the outside but a softie on the inside, so much like you. But you know that. Sometimes she took a maternal role in my life.'

'Yeah, she mothered me, I got away with most things, but not *everything* with her.'

Viola envied the sibling relationship between her father and his baby sister. She yearned for such a relationship with her aunt in her adult years, but fate had its way.

Placido turned off the spotlight and place his hand on Viola's arm.

'Good night sweet aunt.'

They wandered back to the cottage arm in arm, silent.

A rustle in the garden caught Viola's attention and a silhouette scurried off the lawn.

'Papa... look...'

The figure walked towards them. Viola stiffened.

When the person was out on the footpath, Placido burst out laughing.

'It's Alonso! What are you doing out in the garden at this hour?'

Alonso's furtive glance at Viola and hurried explanation perplexed her.

'Mr Bardo, Ms Bardo, I apologize for startling you both. I needed a bit of air and took a stroll through the garden and forgot the time.'

'Well, you are lucky the policeman on watch did not grab you. One wonders if he is sleeping on the job!'

'He knows my midnight jaunts. I come out in the rain too. The officer understands that creatives go out in search of inspiration at odd hours.'

He had an artist's privilege that nobody else was allowed at Galleria Bardo. Viola studied his half-lit face under the footpath lamp. He made no eye contact, and his words flowed after his rude silence at dinner. She had to cut through police red tape before being allowed back into her father's gallery.

Alonso, a visiting artist roamed free on her father's property, close to midnight, with no questions asked when a investigation was underway!

12

Viola was up early to maximize her waking hours with her father before she headed off to her night class.

The odd encounter with Alonso stepped up her urgency to speak to him without appearing curious about his jaunt in the garden last night. Barefoot and still in her night-shirt, her hair in a knotted ruffle, she busied herself in the kitchen hoping to have breakfast ready before her father was up. Placido breezed in five minutes later with the same intention to spoil her with a surprise lavish breakfast.

'You should have slept-in, meu filho. What are you making? Peanut brittle, hmmm?'

'Getting up early is in my blood. No, not peanut brittle! I'm weaning myself off it, to be honest.'

'Why? You love it! We only live once! Ha! But I know women are always following some health fad or the other.'

'It's not a fad papa. As I get older, I appreciate good health. You should too. I feel so much better for having cut back on my sugar intake. Too much every day, catches up with you.'

Her father indulged her, never wanting her deprived of

anything she enjoyed. In his eyes she would never grow up. Her recent health setbacks remained private. This would compound his stress in these troubled times. He encouraged his Artista's love for *caramello* popcorn and Lorenza developed her love for peanut brittle.

'I need to watch my weight, especially because as women age our metabolism slows down and many ailments creep in.'

'Weight? You must be joking! Look at you, you are so thin, like you have been starving yourself all this time. You need to be living here full time so I can fatten you up. You are the skinniest Bardo I know.'

Viola guffawed and unending tears streamed down her cheeks.

'Papa, we only know two Bardo's! You and I!'

She cracked up again in a crescendo of belly aching laughter.

'Oh, Artista, how wonderful to hear your laughter reverberate through our home again!

She rubbed the top of Placido's shiny head and knocked him three times on his bald spot with her knuckles.

'Now those feathers, *toque de peñas*, are not peanut brittle! Such tiny knuckles, soft and floating on my head!'

Placido bellowed again until he wheezed, and teared. Viola put her fingers to her lips to curtail their raucous laughter.

'Papa, the artists, if they are within earshot, will think we are a crazy father and daughter! That will ruin our credibility! Gone in an instant!'

'Every artist is a little crazy so don't worry!'

They giggled more and recalled the days when Helena would chastise them for their unrestrained laughter.

'Now on a serious note, Artista, with this new health regime and weight loss business — have you found love?'

He peered at her from the corner of his eye, knowing that she hated such questions.

'No, not yet, but soon I hope.'

Placido frowned, searching his daughter's face for a tell-tale sign.

'You will tell me first who the person is?'

'If, and when someone arrives, you will be the first to know, always, I promise.'

Viola was awkward with questions on love and steered him away from probing into such matters of her heart.

'Crumpets or muffins this morning, papa?'

'I have croissants in the freezer, we can put those in the oven. They are delectable with a generous dollop of butter.'

'No, muffins it shall be, heart health remember!'

'You think I'm too fat?'

'I did not say that! I said heart health. Don't put words in my mouth or play that guilt trip on me! You want me living here with you permanently? I am a nightmare when I make my mind up about something.'

'Oh yes, I know! But it would be a good nightmare to have you living here, so I can see your beautiful face everyday.'

'Ah you say that now, what about after six months of nagging? How about you spoil me with your wonderful coffee?'

'One large pot of freshly brewed coffee coming up!'

Viola said nothing about limiting her coffee intake. A large pot of brewed coffee meant many mugs per person!

'Thank you, papa, let me give you another one of those, as you say, *toque de peñas*.'

He accepted her three taps on his shiny bald patch with the docility of a pony. The morning was perfect, but beneath it, she was uneasy.

She planned to engage with each of the artists on their own. This was the only way to detect what they might have avoided saying in company. Her typical rigid adherence to rules fell away in her intimate connection to the alleged crime. She would sneak back to the gallery undercover, if she had to, to search for the truth. Someone knew more than they were letting on. Family justice had no boundaries. She would crack open each one to reveal what they might be hiding. The truth was necessary to help her father out of a mess he had not created.

Placido excused himself to finish up a project. It would take at least two hours. Viola knew from one creative to another she might not see him until much later in the afternoon.

The time was perfect for an undisturbed chat in the garden with Crystal who was taking in a bit of rare sunshine.

'Good morning, Crystal, enjoying this beautiful floral area of the garden?'

'Oh, Ms Bardo, hello. It is so pretty out here. Your father seems to love roses as much as I do.'

'Viola, please, no need for formality, we are like family here.'

She studied Crystal's reaction. She had to win her confidence for her to reveal all she knew about the other artists.

'Thank you. I am sure you had a lovely evening with your father. It's a great pity that you have restrictions imposed on when you can see him.'

'I did, thank you. I detest the restrictions but will do whatever it takes to protect my father and his reputation. Something strange occurred last night, on our stroll around the grounds.'

There was no point in wasting time on small talk. She needed the truth as soon as possible.

'Oh dear! Was there an intruder on the grounds?'

Viola jumped right into the moment to tell Crystal how Alonso had startled them on his late-night ramble.

'He is a dark horse, the only artist we don't really know much about.'

'I noticed his disconnection during our conversation at dinner last night.'

Crystal stared at the rose bush in front of her, her brow crinkled.

'Alonso used to chat with Voltaire, I observed them deep in conversation a few times and admired that. Men, more particularly artists, often work in solitude, so seeing their friendship was good.'

'So, he connected with someone. I took him for the solitary, gloomy artist type and let his incommunicado pass.'

'All the cottage windows face the garden. I did not pry, but with my curtains drawn back, I have a wide view of the outdoors as the middle cottage. That is how I saw Alonso and Voltaire in several discussions in the garden. Please don't think I'm a nosy person.'

'Not at all! Perhaps they were collaborating on some artwork.'

Crystal scanned the grounds, nervous that someone might hear her.

'I should get back, I have a piece to complete.'

Viola watched her hurry away. Why did she start something significant and then shy away from it?

She prepared for her evening class, and had to leave the gallery no later than 4:30 pm to pick up her teaching folder and take her usual stroll to the college. Crystal's revelation lingered, leaving her unable to concentrate on her preparation. What was the connection between Alonso and Voltaire? She tried to link the pieces — Voltaire was a prolific street artist in his day — Mural Man had a fascination for street art and seemed to follow her — Alonso knew something! Her instinct clung to that.

She had to get inside the warehouse somehow. It was a fortress.

The rest of the day passed in quietness. None of the male artists ventured outdoors.

Nocturnal Alonso was in hibernation.

She scratched in the fridge for last night's leftovers and made a cup of coffee. The temptation was too great with the collection of coffees that adorned her father's pantry.

At 11:30 am a new police officer arrived on watch duty. Viola decided that a casual chat with him would not upset Placido.

The officer stood like a sentry — upright, back rigid as a pole and head inclined forward with his chin raised. Viola wondered if he stood in that position all day and ended up with a crick in his neck, or was his neck already fixed in that position from all the watch duties he did! She opened the gallery door and there he was, statue still with not a hair out of place.

'Good day officer! I'm Viola Bardo, Placido's daughter.'

She extended her hand and remembered the changing of the guard at Parliament House in Athens. She looked into the lined face of experience and unexpected hesitant eyes.

Without a smile he shook her hand.

'Officer Jardine, nice to meet you, Ms Bardo. Are you enjoying your stay with your father?'

The tips of his pointy ears were blood red, but he had the decency to engage with her. None of the officers on watch acknowledged her.

'Yes, it is good to be here to help my ailing father.'

She made a point of stressing that her father was unwell. Officer Jardine looked the sensitive, empathic sort.

'It must be tough on him — the situation here, and no movement to resolve it.'

'Do you have any idea if there will be a shift in the investigation soon?

'Can't say, I have not had a briefing on where things are at this stage. With the holidays here, I doubt we will have any fresh evidence until early in the new year. Although, a man loitering around the street murals was taken in for questioning. But whether that has any bearing on this case is unknown.'

Viola liked the chatty Officer Jardine. He had dropped a pearl she was not expecting to receive.

In under two hours she knew that Alonso had a connection with Voltaire and if her intuition served her right, Mural Man was in police custody for loitering.

Were the wheels of justice oiling up?

13

Tony was not in class.

Viola secretly thanked her lucky stars. She could get away at the end of the two-hour session without Tony's probing questions.

As much as she knew she was ill prepared, she had to go to the warehouse to understand what Mural Man was doing in the building.

Was he called in for questioning at the station? Could a person be detained for loitering, or was there something else...

After class she made a hurried departure, keen to check if Mural Man was on his nightly jaunt back to the deserted side of town.

She buttoned her overcoat down to her knees to keep out the brutal chill. Viola scanned the streets with all her senses primed for a glimpse of a long, swishing coat. Much to her dismay a light drizzle started, fuzzing her field of vision. Determination pushed her to continue the trudge along the quiet cobblestone streets.

Two-thirds of the way into the haunted side of town and

there was no sign of Mural Man. Disappointment, anger and concern collided. Was he in police custody, had he just not ventured out tonight, or could he be ill? It bothered her that she was concerned for his welfare — this wayfarer of the night who wandered into her world by some strange collaboration of fate. His abrasive attitude at their first encounter disturbed her. Now she was desperate for a sight of him, to know he was safe. His eyes beckoned, those familiar unknown eyes.

She trekked back to the waterway to check if he was under the bridge. Smokers gathered in seclusion to pollute the air, but tonight not a soul loitered there. The stillness on the street amplified the hollow clicking of her boots. Anyone could hear her approach from a mile away.

Close to the warehouse, she pulled back into the shadows. Old light bulbs emitted a dusty, yellow light lower down the street. She huddled behind a building across the street from the warehouse and peered from behind a wall, hoping Mural Man would appear. The top floor had a single tiny shattered window. Could he be watching her from the darkness within? She shivered and tightened her scarf.

Half an hour later her legs were wooden after the light rain turned into a downpour. It was a sign to leave. She moved away from the wall, then darted back when she heard the creaking sound of the tired warehouse door.

A doubled-over figure emerged through a narrow gap.

It was not Mural Man!

The hunched, stout man slowly raised his head, looked left, then right, and left again. He looked left and right one more time, and turned crouching back under the half-raised door and disappeared. Viola heard the loud clanging of the door on the uneven concrete, and then silence, except for the splash of rain in puddled potholes that dotted the street.

She waited for ten minutes before she began the cold, wet

trudge home.

A wasted night, but Officer Jardine's words and her gut told her that Mural Man was in trouble with the law. The hunched figure added another mystery on who he was and why he was there.

* * *

Sᴇʙᴀsᴛɪᴀɴ's ᴘʜᴏɴᴇ rang off three times.

Viola gave up and prepared a light dinner of grilled salmon, a microwaved jacket potato and steamed frozen vegetables. She was pleased with her diet regime after the dozens of pizzas she shared with Sebastian. The only time her dizzy spells appeared now was when she got out of bed. No more legs flying in the air in her jump out of bed! Her father would fret, and her mother would scold and have her take every test medical science had invented with blood tests that would leave Dracula starving!

Where was Sebastian when she needed him? She flicked her phone open several times.

From her early days of online training with Tempest, she knew how important being in communication with a teammate was when the pressure mounted. Two heads were always better than one. She appreciated this after her first assignment with a partner. Impatience was not her trait, but under personal pressure, it emerged in her desire for closure for her father and the artists in lockdown with him. Her chakras needed realignment to move forward.

Her daily journal was a tell-all web of her emotions and dark thoughts. She craved structure. Not having a piano or guitar to soothe her agitation, and with poetry on a sudden hiatus, she had to frame her course of action. At the top of the page she wrote the date, 19 December, and once her pen hit the page, her thoughts tumbled out as her to-do-checklist:

* Find out where Mural Man is now.

* Go inside the warehouse

* Sneak into the gallery without papa knowing to listen in to the conversations the artists are having.

She added in at the bottom of the page:

* NB: this is the way forward now — it is too close to Christmas. I need answers!

She left her journal open on the dining table when her phone rang.

'Hi Sebastian!'

'Sorry for taking a while to get back to you, I was at the vet with Jasper.'

'Why, what's happened to him?'

'He's been unwell, not eating and lethargic. He's on meds and boy oh boy it's a mission to get him to chew them!'

'Poor Jasper! Pop the pill in a slice of cheese or chocolate and I promise he will gulp it down. Puppies are like human babies and need coercion to do what is good for them. It's like having a child living with you.'

'You can say that again. I did not expect it would be this much work! His hair was falling. The vet thinks it's psoriasis with the stress of being abandoned.'

'Fur babies are more human than you think. Take a few days off work to give him some TLC.'

'Are you serious?'

'A hundred percent! Nurture him like you would a child.'

His silence jolted her! She trod on a sensitive part of his own childhood — his feelings of abandonment. It was too late. She had said it with no malice, but he felt the barb.

'I should get that I know. I do not need a crash course on being a good parent! Now tell me what is happening at the gallery. Did you have time to extract information from the artists?'

'I had extended time with my father thanks to Tempest.'

'Our Tempest, she amazes me with what she can pull off! Go on.'

'I gathered two bits of interesting information. The significant part is, as gathered from the police officer on duty, a person loitering around the murals is in police custody. The other bit is that the artist, Alonso, was close to Voltaire, the missing street artist.'

'Do you think the loiterer is Mural Man?'

'I love the way you say my nickname for him with such ease — like you've met him! I don't know at this stage. I went to the warehouse today, but there was no sign of him. A man, older man, I think, opened the warehouse door as though expecting someone to arrive at that time.'

Sebastian digested each piece of information, segmenting it in his mind.

'It is speculation on our part that Mural Man is the vagrant in police custody.'

Viola cringed at the *vagrant* label he attached to Mural Man. It took a mountain of self-control to stop herself from correcting Sebastian.

'True.'

'I reckon, get Tempest onto it right away for confirmation.'

'I won't get a reply until tomorrow morning. Are you able to intervene for me? Get her to call me.'

'Yes, I can do that, but you must stay awake for her call, it's late there now.'

'Done! I need this info like yesterday!'

* * *

Tempest called at 2 am.

'Sorry to disturb you at this ungodly hour, but Sebastian insisted I get to you before you headed out in the morning. He says you are anxious about this Mural Man.'

It was startling how well Sebastian could read her from that distance. She thought she concealed her concern.

'The news I can share is that police took him in for questioning but have since released him, as at 11 pm, your time.'

'Thank you so much. But that's bizarre that they let him out at 11 pm when the grouse appears to be that he was on the streets at night.'

'Well, there's some method in their madness. They have been following him.'

'Yes, you're right.'

'What's your next move?'

'I plan to get inside the warehouse.'

'You need back up girl! You don't know who or what is inside that building and whether you will leave it alive.'

'What do you propose I do?'

'Do you still have the listening chip I sent you in Athens?'

'Yes, ma'am I do.'

'Please place it in your wristwatch and turn it on when you are inside to allow Sebastian and I to offer you cover. I know this case is your baby, but I do not want any harm that is preventable from my end to befall you.'

'Thank you very much. I will definitely do that.'

'How do you plan to get inside the building?'

'I'm working on that now.'

'Good luck, stay in close touch, get some sleep. You need it!'

Sleep was not Viola's elixir that night, thoughts churned and poetry returned to her troubled mind.

How will I enter hidden
chambers and caverns of your mind?
stealthy catlike pouncing
what secrets will I find?

1 4

At 4 am Viola's backpack was ready with a bag of
walnuts, three apples and a large bottle of water. She
pulled a black skullcap over her curly locks and
tucked in the wispy bits. A beanie rolled over the cap gave her
anonymity. Her tights, hooded jacket and running shoes armed
her for what lay ahead.

Her father's integrity would not be left in the hands of
police. Trust was never her first option — she checked and
double-checked everything before she relaxed her privacy. This
was the reason she shunned close connections. Her own
company promised safety. Tempest in her cyber-way had
become a trusted ally, as did Sebastian in recent months.

Her light-footed silhouette floated down the street to the
derelict warehouse. The city was deserted. No prying eyes as
she slinked down the streets, once a place of great joy, now
turned dark with Galleria Bardo under attack.

At 5 am she entered Mural Man's street. The warehouse
was an eerie tower against the purple stillness of the sky. The
aroma of baking bread followed her from the town center.

Memory returned of the days when she would sit in the back of her father's car on his drive to the bakery. Before they got home, she nibbled the ends of the freshly baked French rolls. Placido knew the temptation of the aroma and fluffy texture of the crisp on the outside, cloud heaven texture on the inside was hard to resist. He propped the brown bag with warm bread within her grasp. Memory was a strange beast when it surfaced under duress.

At the back of the building adjacent to the warehouse, she leaned against the wall. Her skull cap pressed down on her ears and muffled sounds. With a deft flick of her left hand she yanked it off and rolled her hair into the beanie.

She observed the building with unwavering vigilance.

Her cheeks stung in the frosty morning air. She stifled the urge to cough. At five forty-five she activated her listening device to keep Tempest and Sebastian connected for fast action if she was in trouble.

On cue, at 6 o'clock the warehouse door creaked open. The sound seemed labored this morning. It stopped a quarter of the way up and a figure crouched from under it.

Mural Man! He was back as Tempest said!

She watched his lop-sided bounce as he moved down the street. The roller door was ajar. At this hour, the occupants seemed to think there would be no unauthorized entry into the building. With cat-like stealthiness, Viola bolted across the street and dove under the warehouse door. Her foot knocked something over and a quick torchlight flash from her phone revealed stacks of cardboard boxes lined up on the warehouse floor. This was a place of business, a packaging depot perhaps.

A whistle floated over the boxes. She crouched low, barely breathing. It was the melodious whistle of someone busy at work. It was dark outdoors on this cloudy morning, and shadows hindered her peripheral vision. Sound in this dark space was her guide. Lopsided footsteps returned. Mural Man was back! The smell of fresh bread wafted into the dank warehouse with him. Then the rusty door shut in an ear shattering clang when it collided with the chipped concrete floor. A few clicks and another door behind the cardboard boxes squeaked open and banged shut.

Silence.

Who was in the building waiting for the freshly baked bread? Did Mural Man's family live in this hellhole?

Viola sat on her haunches waiting for light to break to scout out what was behind the tower of cardboard boxes. She dared not move for fear of toppling them over. Once she had clear vision, she could manoeuvre her way around them to investigate what lay behind the inner door. It was time to text Sebastian.

Inside the warehouse now.
Waiting for light to snoop around.
All systems on!
Gotcha

She felt safe knowing he was listening in.

Daylight crept over revealing a dim view of cardboard boxes stacked in rows along the entire floor surface with a narrow passageway between each row.

The inner door opened, and Mural Man wobbled to the opposite corner from her. A roasted aroma of coffee brewing filled the air. With no electricity in the building she assumed there was a generator for specific purposes such as brewing coffee! The hunched man she saw the previous night, stood behind him.

'Temperamental princess! My coffee was not good enough for her!'

'Humph!

Mural Man was not a man of many words.

'Let us get rid of her, she's useless anyway, these young ones always are!'

Mural man raised his hand to halt the hunched man, and she heard him growl through clenched teeth.

'No!'

'No need to get upset, I suppose I will have to put up with her rubbish!'

'Do that.'

There had to be a surveillance system in the warehouse because the outer door raised just as Mural Man approached it. If she found the wiring, she would temporarily disconnect it to snoop around without being detected. Mural Man rummaged through a box then followed the hunched man back through the inner door. She craned to see what was behind the door. In what appeared to be a long narrow kitchen, she caught sight of a bright vacant area beyond it. Natural light filtered into that space. There was no movement apparent.

When she stepped close to the door, it swung shut.

Could this be a shipment depot? Cardboard boxes were a clear sign that something was packed and stored. She had to find out what it was and what purpose it served. Anything that could lead her closer to the situation at Galleria Bardo was worth the risk. Viola videoed the interior of the warehouse and sent it off to Tempest and Sebastian.

A stillness fell over the warehouse again.

Half an hour later she heard muffled voices, speaking at the same time. There was a fracas going on when a woman's raised voice conveyed her resistance. Could it be the princess who wanted a special brew of coffee? The voices died down.

Locked in the main section of the warehouse she had the day to contemplate how to get through the inner door. She cast her eyes over the ceiling, searching for concealed cameras. Nothing was visible to the naked eye. Viola reached into her backpack for the surveillance detection device to expose the location of hidden cameras. She sent a message to Sebastian to be silent on their open line. If there was a camera, radio frequency might tamper with her call. She walked around the warehouse, feeling the walls as she went along. When she got near the inner door, she heard a male voice and rushed back behind the cardboard boxes. The wires had to be found if she hoped to get inside the anteroom.

Getting out of there posed a risk if her movement was picked up.

It was time to activate the link that would allow her to locate and deactivate the camera. Her options were to find the surveillance camera or slip out before it found her. Sebastian, her cyber ally had her covered to exit the building. A covert operation was going on in this forgotten broken-down building and she wanted to know what it was. Judging from the timing of Mural Man's nightly walks; that would be approximately how long it would take for her to get away, although his limp slowed him down. She would sprint out of there in half the time.

Her father sent her a text message asking if he could call her. The only way to detract him was to say she had a migraine and needed to rest. Her father, plagued by migraines all his life, dispensed his generous empathy as a fellow sufferer — she was off the hook.

Next to a large toolbox, she found a small block of discarded wood and a rasp. Ready cut wooden planks stood up against the wall.

Viola spent the afternoon filing down a piece of wood to keep the door wedged up when it opened to make her rapid escape.

At 9:30 pm, the inner door creaked a sonorous warning that somebody was stepping out. This was the time she saw Mural

Man on the street. His swishing coat gave off the familiar smell of burned wood as he passed her, hidden behind a stack of boxes. The worst thing that could happen now would be for the boxes to topple over!

The roller door groaned as it raised. Once he was out on the street, and she heard his footsteps fade, Viola wedged the shaved wood in place to keep the door ajar.

She was ready to make her getaway once Sebastian gave her, the all-clear.

15

Viola sat tight.

Five minutes later she received Sebastian's message.

The coast is clear. Hurry out now!

He covered her from that distance via a geo webcam of the deserted street. Motion detection enhanced by his sophisticated equipment allowed him to see Mural Man's movement. Tempest was the mastermind behind the advanced zooming in add-on device he used. When Viola was dubious about its effectiveness, he told her she needed to trust Tempest's computer engineering skills and his ability to ensure her safety.

Trust issues always surfaced when she was challenged. It was something she never resolved after her parents' breakup. Her mother was irate when her class teacher suggested her daughter needed counseling to learn to trust again. The ever ready trusting Placido did not know he was being duped when

Helena was seeing another man. Her demand for a divorce shocked him.

In his years of denial and hope that she would return, Viola saw her father crumble, and slowly the seeds of distrust grew within her. She recalled the lovely Maria, hospitality mistress at Aurora, and how it took a long time before she felt a level of comfort with her. Then she disappeared without an explanation. Viola was not there long enough to delve into what happened to her. She disconnected her number or blocked Viola's communication. Bah! So much for trusting anyone, least of all someone she met recently.

Viola crawled on her belly, swishing her hips side-to-side to gain momentum, centipede style. She felt the cold, concrete dampness on her tights. The drainpipe created a fetid pool that she had to crawl through. It soaked through to her skin.

'Yuk!' she moaned under her breath forgetting that Sebastian was on the line.

'What is it?'

No response.

Once she cleared out to other side of the street, she heard him again.

'Get out of the area now, the door is not fully closed, you must have left the wooden wedge still in place. Get out Viola!'

'I have it in my pocket, I can't understand why the door did not slam down.'

'Stop talking and leave now!'

Viola pulled her hood over her head and ran as fast she could even though her knees ached from crouching for so many hours. Her energy levels were pumped with the adrenalin rush to get away.

In the city center, she rerouted, taking the long way back to her apartment. She knew Mural Man walked along the waterway, stopping under the bridge to talk to a few people — it would blow everything if he saw her.

The sight of the apartment block lights was welcome, but when she entered the foyer, she felt the little hairs on the back of her neck stiffen. Expecting someone to lunge at her from behind, she made a beeline for the elevator and sighed when the doors pulled together.

Someone was watching her.

Her sixth sense was spookily accurate, but she willed it away as she did in her childhood anxious moments. She looked at the park from the landing window on her floor. It was a starless night. After blinking a few times, she knew she saw someone move into the shadow of the old tree. The foyer and street facing windows were a fishbowl with its bright florescent lighting.

Whoever was out there was looking right at her!

She called Sebastian once she caught her breath, blurting out that Mural Man was following her and might have known she was in the warehouse, hence the roller door was ajar after she left the building even though she took the wooden wedge with her. Her uncontrolled anxiety surprised him. Back in Athens she was calm and collected. Nothing threw her.

'You are exhausted from being in the warehouse for the entire day. Get some rest and we can talk tomorrow.'

'Please don't think I'm overreacting. I know what I saw. It had to be Mural Man watching me from the park across from here.'

'I don't doubt that you were being followed but I cannot fathom how it could be your wandering man when I had him tracked throughout the time you were heading back. Now he is almost back at the warehouse door. I am tracking him as we speak. The suspended door will be of some concern to him and the occupants.'

'I don't know, but it felt like it was him although he was a silhouette in this black night. I might avoid going out for a jog tomorrow.'

'Don't stop your routine. That will create suspicion if you are being watched. If you feel you are in danger; I suggest you go out when it is light.'

'You are right, I will sir!' she laughed, relieved to hear Sebastian's common sense.

She calmed down and contemplated how this would all end, and whether the missing artists would return. Poetry poured onto her pensive page.

Galleria Bardo — papa's Taj Mahal
to his darling Lorenza
sibling love locked in eternity
now unknown entities rattle at the door

WORDS DID NOT FLOW AS EASILY as she hoped. She would revisit it in the morning.

* * *

VIOLA WAITED for darkness to lift before she went out for her morning jog. She had to maintain the routine of her exercise regime, and Sebastian urged her not to stop. She felt energetic and positive — she could conquer anything that stood in her way.

In the hallway, she heard a door to the left of her front door open. She thought she was the only tenant on that floor. There was no movement other than hers ever since she arrived.

A young woman dressed in pink flannel pyjamas with her uncombed hair standing on end, peered down the hallway at her.

'Good morning...'

Her trembling voice with fear written across her face, surprised Viola.

'Oh, good morning! I had no idea I had neighbors on this floor.'

The woman stepped out of her doorway onto the corridor.

'May I speak with you, my name's Janice, my boyfriend and I live here?'

'Yes, sure Janice, I'm Viola. Nice to know there's company around here.'

Janice walked towards her, her eyes darting back to her front door, still unsure of herself.

'We moved in a few days ago, you might have been out when we did.'

'Have you settled in? Is everything OK?'

Viola had a knack of getting people to respond to her. If she could get Matthew Soto to warm up to her with his first stony countenance then she could outshine any snake charmer! That is what she hoped was her strength as an investigator operating without the blessing of the law.

'Actually, I've been waiting to hear your door open from 5 am. You go out around that time, but there was no movement from you yesterday, so I assumed you were out. It's comforting for us to know we are not alone on this floor.'

She smiled for the first time.

Viola felt a quickening of her pulse. This young woman was a voyeur into her daily morning ritual... what else had she been watching?

'I went out a little later today.'

Janice could not hold back any longer.

'There was an intruder in the building yesterday morning, a man, he was trying to open your door. My boyfriend disturbed him when he returned home from work.'

'How do you mean, trying to open my door? Did he use keys?'

'No, he was jimmying the door and getting quite frustrated when it would not give.'

'Really?'

Viola's scalp prickled and her jaw tightened. She had not imagined what she saw last night!

'My boyfriend asked him what he was doing and then he lunged at Garrett and pinned him against the wall. I heard the commotion and opened the door. The man was choking Garrett. He reached out and punched the intruder in the face. The man took the fire stairs out of the building. I called the police, and an officer came over and took a statement from us and checked the building. I felt he did not believe us, even though Garrett had red welts around his neck.'

'My goodness! I am so sorry the intruder injured your boyfriend! I have no idea who the intruder is or what he wanted from my flat.'

'The officer said he would get in touch with you for a statement.'

'Nobody has called me. May I speak with your boyfriend?'

'Yes, sure, he's still asleep, I will check now.'

'Don't wake him, I will stay in this morning, come over for a coffee in an hour.'

'I didn't mean to disturb your morning routine, but I felt I should tell you.'

'Thank you very much for letting me know. I owe you and your boyfriend a huge apology. Will you come over with him?'

'Yes, we will. Garrett said he wanted to speak to you. He

knocked on your door several times late yesterday afternoon, but you were out.'

This early morning news left Viola flabbergasted. It could not have been Mural Man. He was in the warehouse the whole time she was there, and she left soon after him at 9:30 pm last night. Was yesterday's intruder watching her from across the street?

At 8 am, her mobile phone buzzed with a call from Placido.

'Artista! Thank God, you picked up! Are you back at the apartment? Are you safe?'

'Yes, papa, I am at the flat. Why are you stressed? What has happened?'

'Martens called me saying the police were looking for you and could not trace you? Where have you been? I told him you might have been out with new friends.'

Viola kicked herself for putting her father through more stress than he already had. She had to come up with a quick plausible reason for where she was.

He told her that someone had tried to break into her apartment. His voice was an echo in her head. While she sat tucked away, crouching behind stacked cardboard boxes, there was a police hunt out for her!

'Oh papa! I am so sorry that you had to endure all this. You are right, I was out with teaching friends from the college. We were out all day.'

Her face burned with the lie.

'Look meu filho, I do not want to pry into what you do with your time. The concern is why was somebody trying to get into your place? The police think you reneged on their orders to remain in the city during the investigation.'

'Investigation? What a load of rubbish! What are they doing about the missing artists? They are already on holiday.'

'I know, I know, the wheels of justice turn in its own time.

You are safe and that is all that matters now. But they must find the person who tried to get into your apartment.'

'I am safe, papa. I will be here all day, but please tell Martens that I am teaching tonight if the police want to talk to me.'

* * *

An hour later there was a gentle knocking at her door and the same hesitant voice.

'Viola, it's Janice.'

Two young nervous faces smiled at Viola when she opened the double bolt. Her eye caught the purple bruise on Garrett's neck. Janice was twitchy and swaying on her feet.

'Please come in. Thank you for coming over, Garrett,' she extended her hand, 'I'm so sorry that the person attacked you while you were trying to protect my place.'

They sat down to coffee in Viola's tiny lounge room.

'Please tell me in as much detail as you can remember about what happened yesterday, more particularly the physical attributes of the intruder.'

'It was around 4:45 am that I was returning from my night shift when I saw the man in the hallway at your door, bending over with a small torchlight, working your door.'

Viola watched his body language for any tell-tale signs of deception. He looked her straight in the eye and continued.

'He seemed an older man, a tad scruffy and smelly like he hadn't washed for a long time. Sorry, I don't mean to be rude about his appearance and hygiene.'

Why did Garrett make that comment, supposedly concerned that the intruder might be someone Viola knew or was close to?

'Please continue, don't spare any details.'

'I knew he wasn't a maintenance man at that hour, and he was using a penknife to jimmy the door. Thank goodness he did not cut me with it. He had a long unkempt beard, so all I really saw were his eyes as he pinned me against the wall. He was strong, but I think he lost his balance when I pushed back while he was choking me.'

'That was a close call, Garrett. I am so sorry. How can I help? Perhaps we could go to a doctor to check out your bruises?'

'I'm okay, but thank you.'

Viola heard enough to know it was Mural Man!

Then Garrett dropped another recollection.

'When he walked to the fire-exit, I noticed his odd gait, like he had an injured leg.'

'Thank you very much, both of you, it means a lot to know I have caring neighbors around me.'

She told them she worked at the local English college part-time and they exchanged telephone numbers to look out for each other.

Now Viola had to wait for her chastisement from the police for being unreachable yesterday.

16

A good teacher worries when her student is away for the third successive day.

Tony's absence went unnoticed at the college.

Viola asked around the class if anyone knew whether he was ill. Glum faces and clicking tongues responded. Nobody cared. It was a dull class when the lively Tony was away. He asked provocative questions expecting an answer and had a knack of putting a smile on any grim face.

Howard stopped calling at her classroom door when she settled into the position.

Tony's absence disturbed her.

She popped over to see Howard after her two-hour session.

'Good evening, Ms Bardo! What a pleasant surprise to have you calling at my door. Everything running smoothly?'

Tonight, his coy smile and flushed cheeks made her uneasy. Had she given him the wrong impression by turning up at his door unannounced?

'Everything is going well, thank you. Although I am

concerned that Tony has been away for three sessions, including tonight's absence, without an explanation.'

Once said, her concern that an adult student failed to turn up to class seemed unwarranted. It was only three classes and now she felt silly for raising it.

'As a schoolteacher I am fixed in my ways in following up on student absence, I suppose.'

Viola's brow moistened when Howard's unblinking eyes implied she was silly to worry. His intensity evaporated, and he looked at her with a twinkle in his eye.

'Missing the charming live wire, I see.'

Embarrassment flushed her cheeks. Dear merciful God, he has the wrong impression!

'No, not for that reason at all! He is keen to finish the course this semester and missing six hours is a sizeable chunk of work. Does the college have a catch-up program policy for absent students?'

His sheepish grin relished seeing her awkward.

'We don't have such a policy for *adult* students who should be responsible for their own learning. Let us wait and see if he turns up to the next session.'

'So, do I go ahead and prepare work for him?'

'Absolutely not! We don't know why he is away, and he may be up to no good. We will feed his ego by playing to him.'

Viola took a second to digest his heartless attitude.

She made a point in her career to reach out to students who fell behind in their work. Howard's attitude was new and shocking.

This was not her way.

With or without Howard's permission she would construct a catch-up plan for Tony.

'It's a good thing you came over tonight. Vanessa Smythe is scheduling a staff meeting next week and needs confirmation of your availability. All staff, including part-time and casual personnel, are expected to attend.'

This was the first forthright directive compared to how everything else was run at the college.

'Let me know when she plans to hold the meeting, and I will be there.'

Another first was the question on her availability to attend a compulsory staff meeting. Rob Dwyer sent out a memo at the end of a week advising staff of up-coming meetings at least two weeks in advance. He had a projected year planner available on the school's portal. Things did not happen when they happened at Blackwater Performing Arts Academy. She missed Rob's structured management.

'Ms Smythe seems to favor Tuesday for her meeting. How does that fit in with you?'

'Tuesday?'

With so much changing around her, she had to recalibrate her days to be sure she was available and not over committed.

'Yes, that should be fine, please let Ms Smythe know I will attend.'

She thanked Howard and wondered why she thanked him for doing nothing to help her understand why Tony was away. Gratitude was engrained by her father but wasted on those consumed by self-importance.

Out on the street, she was vigilant to all movement around her. The park, across from her apartment was quiet except for an old man walking his reluctant dog. Dogs had a mind of their own and gave in to their whims as much as children did. She swiped her entry access card and jumped in surprise when someone called out her name.

A smiling Garrett approached her.

'Good evening Viola, sorry, did I startle you?'

Her head swirled with the speed in which she spun around in response to his voice.

'Oh Garrett! How are you?'

Her eyes darted to his neck. The purple welt was gone!

He noticed her surprise and pulled his scarf around his neck.

She was not going to pretend she did not notice this surprising detail.

'Your bruise has healed in a day, that's amazing!'

'I scar easily, have always since I was a child. It must have been a superficial one. The pharmacist prescribed an ointment which did the trick.'

Viola smelt deception in his instantaneous conjuring. Her intuition, known by her students, fired her pursuit of hearing nothing but the truth.

Garrett shifted the conversation and asked if she was at the college that evening.

'Yes, I was. Are you returning from work?'

'I finished work at eight today, my half-day session. I'm glad to have the evening off. Janice has been jittery ever since the intruder got into the building.'

'I don't blame her, that was scary. Especially when entry to the building is only through a personal access card.'

She studied his body language for signs of guilt.

'Have the police called you yet? Do they know who the man was?'

He was full of questions tonight, offering insubstantial answers to whatever she asked.

'No, not yet, but I'm sure they will get in touch soon. There is no urgency, I suppose. Technically nobody was injured.'

'Except for me, but I am small fry in all of this.'

They chatted in the elevator and parted when Viola reached her flat door.

Her suspicion gnawed. How could he think she would believe that a bright bruise could fade in a matter of hours?

A hot cup of tea was essential tonight to calm her agitation on why this young man lied.

Tempest and Sebastian buzzed.

'Greetings you two! I am in bad need of company tonight!'

'What's made you this desperate to have our company?'

Sebastian teased, enjoying horsing around in typical little brother fashion when he perceived Viola's agitation.

'I know how frustrating waiting for news from the police must be, and boy oh boy, they know how to drag their heels! But for what it is worth, I've arranged for an officer to see you tomorrow.'

'I don't know if I'm ready to see the person but appreciate your help and will talk to whoever calls.'

Sebastian asked if her evening class was going well. She raised her concern on Tony's absence and Howard's nonchalance on the matter, and that Garrett was asking a lot of personal questions.

'Garrett's just a curious young man, don't worry too much about what he says.'

Tempest dispensed with Tony as a non-essential in the case.

'I think he knows what has happened to the missing artists.'

'We can't be certain this early until we have reason to suspect Garrett is devious.'

Sebastian's comment irked Viola in his assertion of Garret's innocence, a stranger, an unknown to him, yet he chose a male edge on the matter.

'How do we account for the magical disappearance of his neck bruise? I think it was a fake scar.'

'Do not let your imagination get the better of you.'

'It could have been a fake one.'

Tempest interjected to halt Sebastian's disbelief when she sensed the tension between them.

'But you must be on your guard at all times with those young newcomers. They can be beguiling.'

Sebastian fell into silence knowing it was wise not to challenge Tempest. Viola was tempted to ask if sisterly advice peeved him.

WHEN HER PHONE rang for the second time, Viola expected it to be the police and let the call ring out. She needed to think and plan before they bombarded her with questions. Her tired eyes needed some shut-eye. She rolled over and fell asleep for an hour.

At 9 am she climbed out of bed. This was the latest she had ever slept in. She stretched, touched her toes for a few rounds and went to the bathroom.

Her phone rang again.

Persistent cops!

Half an hour later she looked at her phone and noted that she had two missed calls from Matthew Soto! What on earth gave Matthew Soto a reason to call her now? She had to have coffee before she returned his call.

The third call annoyed her. She grabbed the phone, expecting to hear Matthew's voice.

'Good morning, Ms Bardo, officer Manning here from the local station. Are you home this morning?'

'Good morning, Officer Manning. I've been expecting your call.'

'Good! May I come over this morning regarding the intruder in your building? I require a statement from you.'

'Yes, please do, but I'm not sure how much help I can offer. What time can I expect you?'

'I can be there in an hour if that suits your schedule. I need all the information I can gather to file the matter, with the holiday season upon us.'

Filed! Right! Not investigated! Just filed!

'I see. An hour makes it an urgent matter, I think.'

Viola bit her lip. She hated being sarcastic, but when civic duty was not given due priority, she turned into a fiend.

Officer Manning hung up without a word of thanks.

She had to get her story straight to avoid any inaccuracies. A few scribbled thoughts helped her to fabricate her whereabouts on the night the intruder came to her door.

1 7

O fficer Manning arrived at ten.

A silvery haired man with large suspicious eyes. He held up his identification tag and reached out to shake Viola's hand.

'Officer Manning, ma'am. Viola Bardo, I presume. Good to meet you, at last.'

'Thank you for being prompt officer. Yes, tis I!'

She laughed in a bid to ward off whatever suspicion he had of her.

It worked! Officer Manning's face widened and brightened in a broad grin so unlike his initial officious visage. A stern countenance must be his public face. His eyes strayed behind her, taking in whatever first impressions he could form before the distractions of his questioning. He said he was glad to meet her, *at last*, as though he had been hunting her down for ages. Exaggeration or a sense of the theatrical did not get her respect. As a child she wanted stories about life not far-off lands and magical creatures. All she wanted to know was how good people fought off the evil doers. Yet with her pragmatic view of life, the creative side bloomed in music and poetry.

'I have freshly brewed coffee ready. Would you like a cup, sir?'

'I'm not a coffee drinker, sorry, ma'am. Tea is my beverage of choice.'

That was a first for Viola. A cop without coffee and maybe a donut? She had to forget the line up of police cars at the drive through at Krispy Kreme. Officer Manning seemed a wholesome man.

'I could make you a cup of tea if you would allow me five minutes.'

'Thank you. I must decline, I've had my quota for the day.'

Quota of tea? Non-alcoholic tea! Was this guy for real?

All Officer Manning was keen on knowing was where she was the day the intruder got into the building and not who the actual intruder might have been.

This early in the morning with one cup of coffee down she found his habit of tapping on his hardcover notebook in an uncontrollable tic, irritating.

'Ms Bardo, you know that you are under strict instructions not to leave the city without police permission. Has your family lawyer, Martens Direito, briefed you on this?'

Her bristles were up.

'Got that the first time when Martens informed me. I have not left Porto. Put that down, please, for the record.'

'Bear with me, Ms Bardo, some of these questions might not be palatable, but I have to ask them.'

'Sure, please carry on. And just for the record, I will be at the gallery with my father tonight.'

She explained that she was out for the day with her colleagues. He seemed satisfied with that but added that if it were necessary, they would verify her whereabouts with the people she named. It was tempting to remind him that she was not under investigation neither was *she* the intruder!

Officer Manning stood up and shook her hand.

'Thank you, Ms Bardo. I might take you up on that offer of tea next time.'

Was there going to be a next time? Why? His grin annoyed her.

He scanned the flat again with his curious darting eyes. What was he expecting to find? A man in the closet, or perhaps under the bed? Could she be harboring the intruder!

She flung herself on the couch, exhausted, after he left, aware that it did not go well.

A cold bowl of oats sat uneaten on the kitchen counter.

It was time to return Matthew Soto's call.

* * *

Matthew picked up on the first ring.

'Viola, I thought you would never return my call! What a relief to hear your voice!'

'Hello Matthew! I am so sorry for not calling sooner. How are you and little Jungen doing? How is Bernice?'

'We are well, thank you, but my mother has returned to New York. She had some matters to attend to. It's just me and the boy now.'

She was surprised his mother had returned so soon. A thought nagged on whether his call was to ask her to take up an au pair role again.

Lengthy silences punctuated their conversation with Viola scratching her head on what to say next. Working for him was a very formal arrangement until she left Athens. His out of character emotional reaction to her departure had her thinking of him as a strange man, but her love for Jungen compelled her to stay in touch.

'You are probably wondering why I called you today after our last conversation.'

'I must admit I am a little curious. Is it about Jungen?'

'Well, yes, in a way it is. The good news is that we will be in Porto for Christmas, and we hope we can see you during this time. You mentioned that you were busy when we last spoke, but I figured you must have cleared the decks by now on your commitments with the harking of the holidays. I know you are spending Christmas with your father, but hopefully you can fit us in for a cup of coffee somewhere along the line. The little man is excited about the possibility of seeing you again.'

Viola heard the demand for her time and was sure that amidst his unusual garrulous gush she heard him whisper, *as do I*.

Every fibre of her being abhorred this pressure leveled at her. He knew that she was spending Christmas with her father after almost a year. She fobbed off his suggestion of a visit once before. Now he pretty much told her he would be there for Christmas. She detested his disregard of how precious every moment was with her father. Her affection for the boy melted her determination to refuse him again.

'Where will you be staying in Porto?'

'We will spend a few days in Lisbon, then make our way to you. I've booked at the Pestana.'

'That is a beautiful location along the waterway.'

'Well, perhaps you can take a walk with us along the riverside.'

Viola learned that Matthew was a persistent man who got his way around whatever he wanted. That side of his personality put a question mark on his hope for a deeper connection with her. Independence was everything to her in deciding when, where, and with whom she would socialize. Lorenza told her never to allow others, those who brought no value to her life, to railroad her plans. And her resilience left its mark. Now she was bowing to Matthew's plans to intrude on her Christmas with Placido. For Jungen she would agree, and somehow, she had to let him know it was for the boy.

'Let me know what you think about meeting on Christmas Eve. That should not impact on your Christmas Day with your dear papa.'

Well, that was rather thoughtful of him, but how sure was he that she was going to be available on Christmas Eve. He had no idea that a lot of preparation went into the Christmas lunch! His life was an unusual one. With Bernice leaving so close to Christmas, it said a lot about their family priorities. She presented as a doting mother and grandmother when they met. Who was she to judge mothers, given her relationship with Helena? She tossed out the judgement, it was not her call.

'I will let you know what the plans are, and I will try to see you, although I cannot promise more than that at this stage. There is a lot happening now.'

Matthew was quiet for a second.

'Anything I can help you with?'

'I will let you know if I need help. Thank you.'

She knew she was curt, but she would not talk to him of all people about matters that were private to her father. It was time to change the conversation, it was edging towards being too personal for her liking.

'How are things at Aurora? How is the Prime Minister's son? Does he still come over to visit?'

'Where shall I begin? I am not sure, is my honest answer. I don't know how things are at Aurora College. I no longer work for the Prime Minister, although he allows his son to visit. That keeps Jungen happy, and I am grateful for that.'

'Wow, a lot has happened since we last met. And it has not been that long.'

Matthew was quiet again, and Viola recalled her first interview with him — shadowy Erebus, silent and stoic.

'I had to reorganize my life after my mother left. But change is a good thing, one has to admit.'

He did not answer what she was expecting to hear him say, and she accepted that some things were best left alone.

'Thank you for calling, Matthew. I am looking forward to seeing you and the lad soon.'

'*Thank you* for agreeing to catch up with us while we are there. It will be lovely to see you. I will be in touch. Take care now.'

He snatched her acceptance like the life line he craved, and she knew he engineered the trip to Porto. It was more him, not the boy that needed to see her again.

Viola curled on the couch, warmed by the sound of Matthew's voice. She was not going to allow that to heat up, there were important things beyond his visit to occupy her. Her father had to be told that there might be a minor change to their Christmas plans.

Rugged in a long red scarf, floppy beanie, carrying a large duffel bag, Viola arrived at Galleria Bardo with a song of joy in her heart. It was the coldest evening since her arrival a fortnight ago. The brown paper bag with soft white bread rolls that she tucked under her arm lay flattened in her rush to get home.

The fireplace radiated a soothing glow. Placido's Artista felt colder than most people when winter bit through to her bones. He knew she loved the rain, but the winter chill left her sniffly and miserable. The adult years saw her in stronger physical health, but her winter afflictions remained, chilling her marrow.

The welcome sight of her father doubled over at the fireplace, toasting chestnuts, warmed her after a strange morning with Officer Manning. Her heart sank when Placido tripped, bubbling with excitement in rising to greet her.

'Careful papa! Did you injure your foot on the poker?'

'Artista! I am ok, do not worry. Lovely to see you, meu filho!' He grabbed her hands.

'Dear God, your hands are ice blocks! Where are your gloves?'

'I'll warm up soon. Gloves are a hinderance. It must have taken you all afternoon to get the fire started. You should have waited for me to help you. Are you sure you did not hurt your foot or back? You almost took a tumble there.'

'I will live! You sound like Helena when you fuss over me. Well, more Helena in the younger years.'

His nostalgic look tugged at her. He loved his little family and would have sacrificed heaven and earth to keep their lives intact.

'Here, let me attend to the fire, you can bring the bread rolls back to life by placing them in the oven for ten minutes. Do you still have olives and cheese in the fridge?'

'Yes, they are in the fridge. Yum! These bread rolls smell heavenly. Why so many? Are they from the bakery near the apartment?'

'Yeah, but I flattened them in my rush to get here.'

'I will resurrect them! Never fear.'

His laughter was a sign that he was coping even though he could have been injured with that awkward trip so close to the fire!

'Now would madame like some coffee and marshmallows toasted to perfection or red wine instead?'

'Too many choices! You make it seem like I have just arrived in the country! You are adorable!'

'Oh, stop that now! I only have one Artista and she will have the best.'

'Thank you, papa. Coffee and marshmallows, it shall be! I have had little or no sugar this week, so a little decadence can do no harm.'

'Huh! Healthy eating gone with the wind when you're with your papa!'

'I am allowed one treat tonight, and I might add, which you are shamelessly encouraging.'

Viola loved these indulgent days with Placido. All her worries washed away when she was with him.

'Only for tonight, tomorrow we go back to our promise for healthy eating, living, thinking and breathing.'

'I will hold you to that dear papa.'

His sidelong glance did not fool her. He sensed something was bothering her. It was not often that she went against her healthy eating choices. Something had led her to the bakery that evening for the indulgent purchase of two dozen fluffy white, carbohydrate overkill bread rolls!

'What is going on, meu filho? I know my girl — something is bugging you. Now tell me, I am ready to hear it, even if it takes the entire evening.'

Placido fixed his usual lowered head, steady gaze on Viola, waiting for her to be honest with him. He knew her tendency to harbor secrets in her desire to avoid troubling or hurting anyone. She said nothing more about the intruder at the apartment. He was perturbed that she was internalizing her fear.

'I do have a lot on my mind, papa. You are psychic, as always. I can never hide my feelings from you, you know me too well!'

Viola threw her arms up in surrender to his will.

'Here it is, but please do not judge until you have the complete story from me, promise?'

'Well, I do declare this sounds like an intriguing revelation!'

'I said don't judge. Or I will clam up, you know that.'

'I'm listening, meu filho. I promise not to interrupt.'

'An acquaintance I met in Athens will be in Porto for Christmas. He is hoping to catch up with me while he's here.'

Now it was her time to study her father's reactions, but he said nothing. He sat still looking at her, waiting for more.

'He is coming with a little German boy that I helped with English, while I was at Aurora College.'

Placido was restless, itching to ask a question. In desperation, he raised his hand.

'Now you are my student? Okay papa, ask and I will answer.'

'Is this nameless gentleman coming on holiday with his family?'

'No, he is coming with Jungen, his nephew. Apparently, the little boy has been asking to see me. He is an adorable little fella.'

Placido's eyes were wide, his tongue burning to ask that which might get him on the wrong side of his beloved Artista. Then, like every good father, he stepped headlong into it.

'Adorable little boy? What about the nameless gentleman? Is he adorable too?'

'Don't go there, please papa. His name is Matthew, Matthew Soto.'

'Italiano?'

Viola frowned and refused to comment.

'He lives in Athens?'

'He is American but working, or should I say was working in Athens.'

'Hm ... why is he not working now?'

'I don't know! He is not a prospective suitor, so don't ask me these unnecessary questions.'

'Sorry I'm just being papa, no matter what age you are, I will ask.'

Viola shook her head, knowing it was useless arguing with her father who would never accept that she did not need him to be her knight in shining armor. Whether Matthew was a friend was questionable.

'I sense you are very fond of these people. They will spend

Christmas Day with us and as much time as they want to at the gallery while they are here. Your friends are welcome any time in mi casa.'

'That won't be necessary. Matthew wants to meet on Christmas Eve, so I might go over before I come to the gallery.'

'I insist you invite him and the boy for our special lunch. The more the merrier and it would be lovely to have a child around us. Come on, indulge your papa on this, please.'

'It's not up to me, papa. I will ask when the time is right and let you know. For now, just know that there will be some friends visiting, and I might take out a little time here and there, an hour or so just to be with them. Thank you for always being so kind and generous.'

'No need for thanks, meu filho. It will be good to have new company around us.'

He reached out and pressed her hand. Her father knew something had changed ever since her arrival. She left a part of herself in Athens.

* * *

LATE THAT EVENING, after Placido retired for the night, Viola sent Sebastian a message to ask Tempest to call her. This convoluted communication was the norm if she was not on assignment with Tempest. It was a safe option while the gallery was under police investigation. Police would be watching her. Technology was not her strength as her intuition was. It never let her down.

She had to ensure that Tempest approved this request of friendship from Matthew Soto. Matthew was part of Tempest's investigation for the late German ambassador when Jungen disappeared from their home. The last thing she wanted was to irk Tempest. Sebastian had a taste of her wrath!

Overthinking outcomes were part of her investigative process, but sometimes it made her anxious when negative possibilities took precedence. What if Tempest discouraged her from seeing Matthew? How would she explain this to him?

Tempest's call came in at midnight after hours of playing out various scenarios that yielded no answers.

'Viola! How are you? Sorry for my late call again, but it has been a hectic day. Everything going as expected — any hiccups?'

'Thank you for calling. Things are slow on this end. Awfully slow. A situation has arisen, but it is unrelated to the gallery.'

'What is it? Don't leave me hanging. It's late enough on your end, so quit the dance.'

Viola felt her stomach coil. This did not get off to a good start! She had half the mind to avoid talking about Matthew at all.

A few deep breaths stopped the coiling in her belly.

'I had a call from Matthew Soto. He will be here for Christmas. '

'How is that a situation, as you say? What does he want?'

'He wants to see me, it's a social visit.'

'What do you need from me?'

Viola felt admonished for asking a silly question, or for wasting Tempest's time.

'Are you going to ask for permission to see him? See him is all I can say.'

That came straight from the oracle, and Viola was ready to dance in relief.

'I felt it was appropriate to ask because the case in Athens was your elected investigation.'

'That case is closed. Done and dusted. This is your personal business.'

'Thank you Tempest.'

'Do as you please. It seems Mr Soto has taken a fancy to you.'

Viola heard Tempest's husky laugh on the other end of the line, and fear vanished like a fleeting apparition.

Tempest's next question baffled her.

'If I were you, would I meet him again? What do you think?'

Viola was afraid to step on Tempest's toes with an incorrect response, and opted for silence.

'Hell yes, I would! He is a gentleman in every sense of the word. Let me tell you, I have not met many in my time. So, go wine and dine him, do whatever tickles your fancy! You only live once.'

Her honeyed laugh dripped with a longing for what she never had.

'I don't know if I want to do all of that. Perhaps dine.'

Viola enjoyed the unusual lighthearted conversation, aware of Tempest's nostalgia.

'Is there anything else?'

'That was all. Thank you, Tempest.'

TEMPEST LIT her pipe and walked out onto the balcony. She was pleased that agent Bardo was above every law agent she had encountered. It was a blustery night with icy winds blowing in from the North. Her knees ached. Walking was not an option today.

Khaya and Woza whimpered at her feet, disappointed that there was no run on the beach.

'Shush you two, earn your colors like Viola has.'

Sea spray dampened the balcony. Tempest hauled Khaya and Woza indoors, pulled down the shutters and curled into her armchair with a book. It was not just her knees that were sore, her eyes ached, her heart heavy. She poured herself a glass of red and fell into a lonely sleep after one sip.

19

Baking bread tickled Viola's nostrils. It was dark and barely 6 am. She inhaled the warm smell, put on her track pants and cardigan, and strolled barefoot to the kitchen.

Crystal was bending over the oven and turned on her heel when she sensed someone had entered the kitchen.

'Good morning, Ms Bardo! You surprised me there! I thought I was the only one up and about this early. I hope I did not disturb your sleep with my rattling pots and pans.'

'Far from it, I heard none of that. The wonderful aroma of baking bread danced right down to my bedroom. Like Pavlov's salivating dogs, I followed my nose!'

Her hearty laugh had Crystal taking a deep bow.

'You have the same sense of humor as your wonderful father. You both share such a warm relationship.'

'Why are you up early working so hard in the kitchen? By the look of it, you are preparing enough for the entire team in residence.'

'Mr Bardo is always preparing generous meals for us so I

thought I would surprise him this morning because I know he loves fresh homebaked bread!'

'You know my papa well already. He is a breadbasket! He had an indulgent evening with the bread rolls I brought in last night. What a generous offer of your precious time. Papa will be most pleased.'

'Oh dear, had I known he had bread last night, I would have baked these on another day. Your father has spoken of the amazing bread his mother and grandmother baked when he was a kid. I have watched him when he speaks of them, his face softens and glows in memory of those years.'

'Papa had a great relationship with his mother and grand-mother, but unfortunately they passed on before I was born. I did not have the good fortune of meeting them, but the love for bread has passed through the genes!'

'Everybody no matter where they are in the world loves bread in whatever hue, or shape. In my part of the world we love our flatbread. Buttery soft and flaky or thick and spongy is a perfect accompaniment to a good meal.'

'Well, look at us, this early in the morning, and we have food, glorious food on the brain!'

'It is in our DNA as women!'

They chatted over a pot of coffee with Viola sampling Crystal's delectable poppyseed bread rolls. All intentions on healthy eating were out the window again that morning. She wished her father could have such company around him all year long. He enjoyed his creative solitude, but now at this point in his life, company was necessary to keep him connected.

Crystal's abrupt end to their conversation and uneasiness startled Viola. She followed Crystal's eyes to see Alonso at the kitchen sink. His stealthy entry went undetected by Viola.

'Sorry ladies, please ignore my presence, I came over for a glass of water. Please pretend I'm not here.'

He declined the poppyseed bread roll Crystal offered him, helped himself to coffee, and left without another word.

'What a rude man! Rudeness personified!'

Crystal hissed between clenched teeth.

'It takes different types to make up this world.'

Crystal shook her head, annoyed by his presence.

'He is a closed book. None of the other artists have his disposition.'

'Ah well if he keeps to himself, I don't mind. He can have his solitude and antisocial behavior!'

'I have a distinct feeling *Mr Arrogant Alonso* knows why the artists are missing.'

Crystal's words sent a shudder through Viola.

Could her father have invited an enemy to Galleria Bardo?

Viola pondered over Crystal's speculation for most of the morning. What had she missed in her encounters with the remaining artists? Did Crystal know more than she was letting on? Why is she wasting her time pursuing Mural Man when the answers were right here at the gallery?

Three people could not disappear from the same place without a connection among them. A skillful individual or an organization orchestrated this. She was sinking into something deeper than she originally envisioned.

Viola needed help from Tempest and Sebastian with her research on Alonso. In thinking this through, she had no details to share with them other than his name. His last name was something her father had never mentioned, and now it would make him nervous if she asked too many questions about this artist. Placido was busy in the workroom, which gave her the space to conduct a private perusal through his filing cabinet.

Her father was of a free and open nature. Locking doors

and draws was not his way. Where he trusted with no reserve, she had to have proof of allegiance first.

A struggling sun peeked in through the blinds in his office. As she suspected the filing cabinet was unlocked. Placido was a paper man — literally paper. He turned his back on technology, hating spreadsheets or anything digital. For one who kept an unlocked office, it was ironic that he feared cyberattacks if records were saved in a cloud or hard drive. No amount of trying to convince him would change his ways. All he used was a mobile phone only for emergency telephone calls. A large black dial phone sat on his desk. Everything about his office was a journey back in time.

In the overloaded cabinet, she found a file labeled, *Artists in Residence*, and a flick through the pages yielded a list of the artist's details with their profile photographs attached.

Alonso was Alonso Fernandez! He was forty-two, although he looked much younger in his face and physique.

She had all she needed and was about to leave when she paused to take a photograph of the page with Alonso's picture.

Satisfied with what she found, she shut the cabinet draw and turned to find Alonso standing in the doorway of her father's tiny office!

Her heart revved like Formula 1 engines at the Grand Prix.

'Alonso! I did not expect to see you here. Are you looking for my father?'

His cold, unemotional stare made her tremble. She leaned against her father's desk to steady herself.

'Sorry if I caught you off guard, Ms Bardo. I knew Placido was in the workroom and heard a sound in here and came over to check. You never know with what's been going on around here.'

That was the most he said to her since her arrival at the gallery. Why was he in this part of the building if he was not being nosey? Before she had time to compose herself to read Alonso's body language, Placido popped his head in behind Alonso, his eyebrows arched with questions.

'Everything OK in here, Artista?'

'All good, papa, Alonso surprised me with his sudden appearance.'

'I'll leave you now.'

Alonso hurried out, pushing past her father with no regard. Placido watched him rush away, his eyebrows still arched.

'What brought you to the office, meu filho?'

He sensed her uneasiness.

'I was looking for my earrings. I seem to have misplaced them, but they are not here.'

'What brought Alonso to this part of the building?'

'I ask the same question papa! He is an odd fellow and I would not trust him if I were you. Come now let us go to the kitchen, Crystal has baked you bread. She is a lovely person.'

'An artist working the canvas, and an artist in the kitchen! She sure is a talented lady and has been good company around here. Forget this crazy fellow!'

Viola saw the lonely man in her father once more. She would not talk about Alonso again. They had a pleasant day drifting in and out of conversations while eating too many poppyseed rolls.

* * *

At sunset, Viola left the gallery for her evening class.

An unplanned detour to the laneway where she first met Mural Man tugged her in that direction. With two hours to spare before her class, she felt compelled to cast her eyes again on the second mural that entranced him.

The wall was bold and vibrant against the setting sun.

A woman standing among a cluster of trees had terror emblazoned in her eyes. Behind the woman, a little boy peered over a rock. The woman's hair was wild and wiry, like electricity had passed through her. The wide-eyed child looked terrified. His fingers gripped the edge of the rock with his little face barely visible above it.

The black cloud over the woman added a sinister touch. Was she evil or a victim of evil? The sky was gray above the child. Why was Mural Man obsessed with this painting?

Viola sauntered to the college in a tangle of thoughts. The mural, the man, and her father's situation beckoned for the key to this mystery. Instinct guided her legs to the college entrance.

She heard her name called out somewhere in the distance. Then close.

'Viola! Ms Bardo, wait up!'

She did a three-sixty turn and with a spinning head saw Tony's worried face. His scruffy attire was out of whack with the neat as a pin, polished Tony who came to her classes.

'Tony! Where have you been? I wondered what had happened to you.'

Her heart had the habit of speaking before her brain could caution her. Had she crossed the line of professionalism by speaking to him this way? It was second nature with her high school students to tell them she missed them. Howard's words haunted her.

'Ms Viola, I knew it would only be you who would care about what had happened to me. Nobody else at the college does. None of the administrators called me to find out why I was away.'

'I am sorry to hear that. Shall we go up to class, Tony? You can chat to Howard.'

'No! I cannot come to class tonight!'

He pointed to his disheveled appearance.

'I have some problems to work out, I will return as soon as I have figured out what to do. I came tonight to say thank you for the work you sent to me.'

'Oh Tony, you did not have to come to say thank you. It is my job to make sure that my students are up to speed with the content I am teaching. I don't need to know why you were away.'

'Thank you, thank you.'

He reached out to shake her hand, and Viola hesitated, then accepted his thanks. Tony appeared in need of solace from something that was troubling him. She could not cross that line. The best thing was to hand it over to someone in the administration.

Her face burned in empathy with his situation, something she had no idea about. Seeing a person bent and broken pulled at her heartstrings. Tony's bravado, the feigned ego, the top-notch dressing — all a facade for something buried deep within him. Then he placed her in a greater predicament when he asked for her telephone number.

'That is not possible, Tony. You should understand that I am the teacher and you are my student. Our communication is only through the school portal.'

'I don't want to create any problems for you. I just need someone to talk to, someone who will not judge me, someone who will not think I am a failure. Only you can do that in this place.'

'Sorry Tony I have to abide by the rules of professionalism, I can pass this on to Howard.'

'Rules! Who cares about the rules! They have done nothing but create problems for me.'

'I care about rules. You must excuse me now. I have to get to class, I have students waiting for me.'

Viola walked away, aware that Tony was standing there

watching her. Then she heard him call out as she entered the building.

'Ms Viola, please do not tell Howard I was here tonight.'

How could she not?

She stayed on after class, wrote a report about what transpired with Tony, and emailed the document to Vanessa Smythe.

Alonso and Tony both on the same day!

Viola actioned Crystal's nagging suggestion on Alonso's possible involvement by passing the information to Tempest and Sebastian to investigate the sinister Alonso Fernandez.

Her email on Tony's situation arrived on Vanessa Smythe's desk. It was noted and added to her agenda for the staff meeting.

She arrived at the meeting dressed in formal attire. The staff present were in casual wear. Vanessa Smythe advanced with flailing arms and her customary disjointed gait the instant she saw Viola arrive.

'Ms Bardo, ah we did not send you the meeting dress code brief. It is casual gear on meeting mornings. Perhaps I should get you to chair the meeting since you are dressed for the part.'

She guffawed, sprayed the air around Viola, snorted and walked away.

Viola's beetroot bright face was hard to conceal. This public shaming for her apparent improper attire made her the college idiot in the head's eyes. Why did she make a spectacle of her dress? Rob Dwyer expected formal dress at his meetings. She was out of her depth here, and a quick glance at Howard gave her no hope of saving her dignity. His smug grin was set to stay.

She longed to be back home where nary a crass comment passed Rob's lips. A large black frame on the wall behind his desk bore the Arab proverb:

> *The mouth should have three*
> *gatekeepers*
> *Is it true? Is it kind? And is it necessary?*

The head's comment was both unkind and unnecessary. Viola summoned all the grace she could muster to forgive Vanessa Smythe's unkind crudeness. This was the only way to compose herself. The agenda detailed assessments and examinations before Ms Smythe leaned over and looked Viola in the face to the exclusion of everybody in the room.

'On the subject of Tony, let me say that all contact with him must cease with immediate effect.'

Viola waited, anxious for the reason underpinning this statement.

'He is no longer a student at our college. I cannot divulge the reason for my decision. Immediate cessation of all contact has been mandated by the board. Do you have any questions, Ms Bardo?'

A rock descended on Viola. The board was involved, and she was singled out again and associated with Tony. Tony, the college's apparent bad boy.

'No questions, thank you.'

'Good, now that we have that settled, there are a few issues pertaining to the general housekeeping around the college that requires our attention.'

The meeting was a blur for the rest of the hour as Vanessa Smythe droned on. A wasp out of tune. At the end of the session, Viola left without speaking to Howard or other staff present.

She wandered through the city streets on this unexpected sunny morning. The desire to revisit Mural Man's wall art compelled her to take a detour to the lane. She had to lose herself in its mystery to forget her harsh morning.

At the furthest end of the laneway a cool breeze wafted in from the waterway entrance. With subdued natural light in the space, her eyes took longer to adjust to something gently fluttering at the bottom of the mural with the woman and child. As she got closer, she saw a note affixed to the wall. She unfurled the yellowed lined paper and read:

Meet me here around eight tonight.

No person addressed.

No name attached.

Could Mural Man have left this message for her?

She jumped out of her skin when a large squawking bird darkened the strip of sunny sky in its angry flight.

Viola placed the note back where she found it and decided to return at 8 pm. This meant canceling her dinner plans with her father and coming up with a reasonable explanation for her change to their plans. Martens had negotiated more days for her to stay over at the gallery, and she had to respect the privilege of her limited access to her father. Placido would understand if she said she had college work.

Turning up at 8 pm was a risk to her safety in the isolated, dim laneway with an unknown messenger. Sebastian advised it was imperative for her to have the listening device active.

In her usual undercover dress, black tights, sweatshirt, hooded jacket and runners, she had everything in place for a speedy getaway, should the need arise.

She hovered a distance away from the lane entrance, just far enough to observe who was entering or perhaps leaving and whether the note was intended for her.

At 8:00 pm all was quiet.

Nobody entered or left the lane.

Lighting was poor inside the lane, making the wall art imperceptive.

At 8:10 pm, Viola snuck into the doorway of a cafe when she saw a figure approach.

Tony sauntered into the lane!

Her pulse pounded.

What was he doing here?

Five minutes later, Mural Man tottered in behind him.

She waited a few seconds, then crept closer to look down the lane.

Sebastian listened in, picking up her coding.

'TB and MM in the lane now.'

'TB and MM — Got that — Do not go in — Observe and note.'

Both knew her, one by sight, the other by close interaction. This was risky!

The men were in earnest conversation with their backs facing her. She wished she could hear what they were saying. Then Mural Man grabbed Tony's arm, and both walked out through the waterway exit. Gone! And she was none the wiser about why they met. Viola hung around for half an hour hoping they would reappear and gave up and headed back to her apartment close to 10 pm.

Sebastian called it, *The Tony Connection*. Then he suggested something which confused her.

'You must go back into the warehouse. This time with informed eyes. You will know what to look for. Attempt to get past the kitchen to check out whether whatever is going on in there has any links to the gallery.'

'Something is afoot at the warehouse.'

Tempest jumped onto the live line.

'I've been listening in and it will be remiss of me if I did not say that you put yourself at great peril going to the lane after you saw the note. Did you think it was for you?'

'I suppose I did. I am astounded as I did not expect to see Tony. Do you approve of Sebastian's suggestion that I revisit the warehouse?'

'It is risky but necessary. Sebastian is correct. You might find some detail that you missed the last time you were inside. But Tony's involvement requires investigation. His expulsion from the college is mysterious. I suggest you get hold of his college records first. Do this before you go to the warehouse.'

Viola was uncomfortable about breaking into Vanessa Smythe's office. She had to check the head's rostered days to ensure an undisturbed night in her office.

'Are you prepared for police involvement when you go to the warehouse.'

'Would I need it?'

'If your safety is at risk. Sebastian and I cannot offer physical support with the distance between us.'

'Only if there is potential risk.'

'Come up with a plan and run it by Sebastian and I. Act in the heat. Time is running out.'

Tempest clicked off.

Sebastian was quiet during Tempest's instructions.

'You should heed her advice for police backup, and act swiftly.'

'Yeah but the police cannot know about my meddling in the case.'

'Never fear, Tempest will cover you on that. You are her number one, agent Bardo!'

'Matthew is arriving in three days, so I have to get onto this ASAP.'

Sebastian was quiet whenever Matthew Soto's name came up.

'I will attempt to get into the college files, tomorrow sometime. Once satisfied with what I find I will expedite my trip into the warehouse.'

'Your plan is sound and in motion! Good luck Viola! I will be hooked to you every step of the way.'

'Thank you for supporting me through this.'

'We are a team. One family.'

Sebastian's warmth heartened Viola. Her little brother connection to him was deepening.

2 1

O fficer Manning called with no leads on the intruder. Viola's neighbors who reported the matter to her were scarce in recent days.

The magical disappearance of the strangulation marks around Garret's neck, opened a door of suspicion around his involvement in the attempted break-in. A fantastical fabrication of a miracle rubbing ointment that would put most skin specialists and beauticians out of business! Garrett had to be on a mind-altering substance with that yarn. And the surveillance system crashed the night the intruder entered the building?

Officer Manning had no answers, but Viola was not giving up.

'Do you think the footage was deliberately erased, rather than a system glitch?'

'Not likely, although I won't rule that out completely. But then again if the intruder was a friend of the building manager, suspicion suggests it might have been erased. But it does not seem possible.'

Viola detested these flimsy, circuitous, conflicting speculations dressed in 'buts'. Yet another load of codswallop to cover up inefficiency. The riddles of selective language from those who assume power!

'Thank you for that. I really do not want to pursue this further. The intruder took nothing. So, what is there to follow up? If the building management choose to investigate to identify the intruder, they are free to do so. From my end, the case is closed.'

Officer Manning noted her irritation in the long breath she exhaled.

'Sorry, Miss Bardo, it must annoy you having no answers. I will continue the search for the intruder. I refuse to give up.'

'As I said, I won't be pursuing the matter. I won't press charges, even if you find the person.'

Manning wished her a pleasant evening and hung up.

Viola knew the intruder might well be Mural Man. Her protective instinct exuded empathy. She would do all she could to prevent the police from identifying him.

* * *

EVERYONE ACCEPTED that Tony had left the college. Nobody asked about him, and Howard locked himself in his office, avoiding contact with her.

What a strange place! Too many agendas and secrets.

Viola took the waterway route to her apartment that evening. Nobody was under the bridge, nobody sat around low fires, smoking, and staring into nothingness.

Empty streets suggested that people were in a pre-Christmas preparation lock-down in the privacy of their homes.

When she picked up a few groceries on her way from the college, a somber mood prevailed over the usual cheerfulness at the corner grocery store. A grunted head shake acknowledgement is all she got. Was it just her or did it seem like everyone was set to have a miserable Christmas? There was a meanness that was not there when she first arrived.

Poetry burned for a space on the page.

Christmas Spirit where art thou
in your joy and blessings?
now hidden in dour faces
too lazy to feign good cheer

Urgency pressured Viola to plan a return to the warehouse to understand what was underway in this forbidden place. In an unthinking, preoccupied moment, she picked up her buzzing cell phone to Matthew's voice.

'Viola, how are you?'

'Oh hello... Matthew.'

'I have news, Jungen and I arrive two days earlier than planned.'

She paused to figure out what he expected of her. A cheer or song? Why did he say, *we* when the child was six years old and not a decision maker into their plans?

'I hope this will not cut across your plans...'

How in heaven's name could he think that she was sitting around waiting for him to arrive, that she had nothing else to do?

'I'm not sure, as I said when we last spoke, there is much going on for me now... You probably have your plans, so Christmas Eve still holds as a time for me to see you both.'

His silence spoke of his dissatisfaction that she would not accommodate his change of plans. Silence was his inability to accept that not everything could go his way when he suddenly changed his mind. Why was this trip about seeing her? She had not given him hope to believe that she was keen on a long standing friendship — let alone a relationship with him!

'My papa insists that you join us at the gallery homestead for Christmas lunch. Does this suit your plans?'

She rolled her eyes in expectation of his answer, glad that he could not see her reaction.

'More importantly, are you okay with this arrangement? I know you are spending quality time with your father. Jungen and I won't intrude on this special day.'

The man was insufferable in placing his insecurity at her door.

'It is not an intrusion at all. My papa insists and rarely is there anyone who can change his mind once he has decided who will be at his Christmas lunch table.'

She had much on her mind and Matthew's insistence and neediness agitated her.

'I guess that's settled. Your father wins. Thank you very much for the generous offer. Please thank him in advance for me. Jungen will be happy to know that he will spend Christmas with you.'

How transparent, using the boy to cover his own need to see her. She respected a man who articulated his truth with the honesty of his yearning heart.

He promised to be in touch as soon as he landed, and threw in that he hoped she could squeeze in an evening of drinks, or a coffee morning on the day he arrived.

Viola made no promises on that.

She reminded herself to ask her father to move the grand piano into the living room for a singalong on Christmas Day. The gallery needed some livening up, and she was intent on making the spirit of Christmas alive and joyous in her father's home.

But the holiday spirit had to wait until she had fulfilled her plan for another visit to the warehouse.

Nightmares of Mural Man chasing her down the lane and his strange, yet familiar eyes, broke her sleep.

Tempest promised police back-up when she entered the warehouse. Many officers were on watch at the gallery that it was difficult to pinpoint which one of them would support her inside the building.

It was 11:30 pm when she peered out the window contemplating a walk to settle her restlessness. The dense fog-filled night put an end to that thought. She settled for walking inside the apartment block. Running up and down the stairs for a few rounds might exhaust her and induce sleep with the dual benefit of getting in her daily exercise. She hesitated, then took the plunge, put on her joggers and tights, and hit the stairs. The corridor was quiet. She ran down two flights and stopped at the entrance to pick up the mail sitting in her postbox for two days.

She curled on the couch with a hot chocolate, and flicked through her mail. Junk mail went into a separate pile until a familiar yellowed, grainy page caught her attention. The three word scrawl was in the same font as the note she saw on the mural a few nights ago!

Please help me.

What good was she going to do if she did not know who to help? She picked up the note and held it close to her nose. The acrid smell of old wood, burned wood and ash made her sneeze.

Mural Man with his familiar eyes and smell was the scribe.

Time was running out, she had to get to the warehouse in the morning to confront him.

* * *

At 4:30 am she stepped out onto the street and looked across at the park, expecting familiar eyes to be looking back at her.

Nothing moved in the early morning stillness. Not a rustling leaf, a chirping bird, nor a human on walkabout.

When she passed the mural laneway the hair on back of her neck stiffened. She spun around sensing somebody was behind her.

Nobody.

She quickened her pace sure that she would be attacked in the pre-dawn darkness.

Fog and cold air created shadows around her. She kicked her toe against a cobblestone, tripped, and that was enough to inject her into full throttle to run the rest of the way to the warehouse.

Viola wished she had Sebastian's rear vision glasses for a full view of what was happening behind her. She turned the corner into the warehouse street.

The building stood, innocent and abandoned, yet within, human presence skulked with secrets.

In the first sign of light, she squinted, unsure whether it was her imagination — the warehouse door was half open.

Perhaps Mural Man had set out early on his bread run that morning. She waited behind the building on the opposite side of the street, peering from behind a wall.

Five minutes later she crouched over and did a dash across the street and snuck into the warehouse. A dim light flickered across the tiny kitchen from the unknown room behind it. The kitchen door was ajar.

Nobody was there.

For a second she wondered whether she was being set up.

The place was a bolted fortress during her previous time there. Now everything was accessible.

She crept across the cold cement floor into the makeshift kitchen, pressed against the wall, gliding towards the room at the back. The veins in her neck pulsated in a rhythmic thump. A quick head dart out the open doorway and her jaw dropped!

There was Tony with his back to her, painting.

The image on his canvas was familiar.

Viola crept back into the warehouse behind a pile of cardboard boxes. The door was still half open. She made a run for it as though the place was on fire.

Two streets away from her apartment, she saw the lopsided gait, and swinging arms with a bobbing brown paper bag.

Mural Man was returning to the warehouse.

She unlocked the door to her apartment. Another yellowed, grainy note greeted her from the hallway floor.

The bold charcoal words scrawled across the note read:

What do you want from me?

Now she had absolute confirmation that it was Mural Man who left a note in her letterbox, and under her apartment door.

The question begging an answer was how did he get into a secure building for the second time?

2 2

It was time to talk to Mural Man face-to-face, although it could be at great peril to her safety.

In their first encounter, he was hostile, but she was besieged by the sadness in his eyes.

Viola studied the images of the laneway murals on her phone. What was she missing?

A hidden child, a tormented woman, who were they and what was his connection to the image? The ghostly vision of the child revealed his dark skin and wide-eyed fear.

Did Mural Man see himself as the child?

His obsession with the murals tugged harder now to know who he was, and why he was seeking her out.

* * *

HER ELUSIVE NEIGHBORS had to know something.

She rang their doorbell and knocked several times, mindful to be gentle should Garrett be asleep after his nightshift.

158

The door opened ever so slowly with the person behind the door obscured from view.

A gray-haired woman peeped out from behind the front door, fear obvious in her taut expression.

'I'm so sorry for my incessant knocking. I hope I have not disturbed you.'

'That is okay dear, how may I help you?'

'I'm looking for the young couple who live here. Are you a relative?'

'No... not a relative. I moved in two days ago after they moved out.'

'Moved out? Did they say where they were going?'

'No dear, the young man handed me the key to the flat and the young woman said nothing.'

'I see. How unfortunate, I need to speak to them on a matter of urgency.'

'They seemed eager to leave and rushed me through the details of the place. Who knows with youngsters these days!'

'Thank you for letting me know and once again I'm really sorry for disturbing you. I live two doors down the corridor. My name is Viola.'

'Nice to meet you, Viola. It is good to know there are tenants on the same floor. The young man said there is a nice lady in the building, he must have meant you.'

Viola smiled, unsure why Garrett would think she was a *nice* lady. He left without a goodbye.

'That was kind of him, now if you need anything please pop over to my place. What is your name, ma'am?'

'That is lovely of you. I'm Lenora, Lenora Jones.'

'Nice to meet you, Lenora. You have a good day now'.

Lenora shut the door behind a puzzled Viola. How did so much happen on such a quiet floor without her noticing that a new tenant had moved in? The building was a temporary abode

for wayfarers passing through to other places. A makeshift
home, as it was for her.

Mural Man, Tony, Garrett — were they linked to each
other or was she hoping for a link to tie the tattered pieces.

She drew a large circle and placed Mural Man in the
middle with three question marks around him. Tony had a defi-
nite link to him. She had ocular proof. But Garrett, the girl,
and Alonso, puzzled her.

She scribbled under the large confusing circle:

> *A strange mystery*
> *of unknown history*
> *lift the veil in this city*

Working alone on a case had never left her baffled on how
to proceed. After the Athenian saga, meeting and working with
Sebastian somehow ruined her self-reliance, or was she over the
top in this case because of her concern for her father.

Mural Man's familiar eyes did not connect any dots in her
memory.

She gave in to the need to contact Sebastian, to sound out
her confusion, hoping for clarity.

He listened with no interruptions.

'You should have handed the note to the police. In this way
you protect yourself from whoever the intruder is, and you
strike up a cooperative deal with them. As much as I know your
reluctance to get involved with the police, you do need support
on this matter. Your father's gallery appears to be under an
invisible growing threat. Portuguese police can assist you
without knowing you are a PI.

'Don't say it like that, Sebastian, it makes it seem like papa is connected to this sinister web. You and I know that is far from true.'

'Your sensitivity will overlook obvious details. It's a normal emotional reaction.'

'Thank you for that Mr Psychologist! I do not need counseling! I need your ear to help me pick up the strands of what is going on. I need someone on my side, you know.'

'Which I am, Viola, I am!'

'I get what you're saying but please run it by Tempest if that's what I should be doing. It is not that I do not trust you, I need to be a thousand percent sure that I am doing the right thing. My papa is at the mercy of my decisions and actions.'

'I absolutely understand what you are going through. I will give Tempest a buzz and get her to call you as soon as possible.'

'Thank you, Sebastian, I appreciate that.'

Viola studied the note again. The thick black strokes of a large felt-tip pen had an artistic quality. She picked up the paper and held it up close to her nose. The faint smell of wood smoke was there, but soon it would fade.

She mulled over and toyed with ideas as she packed a bag for her night at the gallery until Tempest called.

She wasted no time on civility.

'Viola, *do* as Sebastian suggests. Hand the note over to Martens Direito. Your safety is paramount. The note implies that there is a direct threat to you. Let him liaise with the police on your behalf to free you from communication with them while you investigate undercover.'

'Thank you, Tempest. That makes sense. There is too much personal risk, I agree.'

'Good, that is settled.'

Tempest danced off into the airwaves in one click.

* * *

At the gallery later that evening, Viola made a private call to Martens. Her father needed protection from her involvement to avoid him worrying over her safety.

Martens' agreed to come over in the morning on a casual visit when she would slip him the note without Placido's knowledge.

She wandered off to the workroom around 10 pm, with the note safely tucked in her pants pocket.

The garden floodlights made night a bright day with the roses bathed in its brilliant beam.

The workroom door was open, as always. Crystal's and Alonso's artwork stood in their respective spaces. She walked up to Alonso's work in progress. His canvas looked complete. It bore his signature in the bottom righthand corner.

Viola's feet froze to the floor. She reached into her pocket and pulled out the note. The hand, the font, and curl of the lettering was by the same hand in her anonymous note! She knew it! The handwriting was an exact match to the note that she saw on the laneway mural the night Tony turned up to see Mural Man!

She sighed with every ounce of air in her lungs. Are the dots connecting or was she allowing her mind to lead her to this conclusion? Why did the note smell of burned wood, of Mural Man?

A quick photograph of Alonso's painting was a necessary exhibit to prove whatever would come down the track. She turned to leave, satisfied that she had a strong lead.

Standing at her left shoulder, breathing in long, quick, audible breaths, was a smiling Alonso.

'Trying to steal my work, Ms Bardo?'

She stared at him, her mouth dry, unable to summon the words in her defense.

'Do you like my work? I wish you would tell me if you did before you took a photograph without my permission.'

The stealthy beast had crept up on her, and Sebastian had said because of her emotional entanglement, she would lose her sense of rational perception and heightened intuition in familiar surroundings.

'Who is the photograph for Ms Bardo? What you just did is intellectual theft. I am surprised. One would assume that the daughter of the great Placido Bardo would never do such a thing!'

His menacing arctic tone sent a shiver through her. She was alone in a closed space, unarmed, caught red-handed. And he was right — it was his intellectual creative property. She had no right.

'You are correct, Alonso. I apologize. I love having beautiful artworks on my phone to look through at leisure. I should have asked. I will delete it now.'

'That would be the right thing to do. But I will leave that to you to decide.'

His voice dropped another decibel — the threat was clear. Viola deleted the image in a quick sleight of hand in a double tap — the image flew off to Sebastian's phone and disappeared from hers.

'That's it! Gone! Here look.'

She held up her phone. He looked away.

'Thank you.'

The twinkle in his eye conveyed his joy in crushing her.

Viola thanked all the heavenly bodies she knew — Alonso did not catch her in the act of matching up the note to his signature. Or did he?

'Good night, Ms Bardo. Sweet dreams!'

He swaggered out the workroom, victorious that he had won over the great Placido Bardo's daughter.

Every fiber chastised her negligence in not shutting the workroom door. If her father was lackadaisical about security, she was no different.

Her head was in a mess as she tried to figure out Alonso's involvement in the case of the three missing artists from Galleria Bardo.

Her meeting with Martens had to be offsite after this bizarre turn.

Now Alonso was suspicious and uneasy with her presence at the gallery. He would watch her like a hawk, ready to pounce on her every move.

She compromised her freedom at Galleria Bardo.

23

Placido was miserable. He coughed, sneezed, and complained about his sore throat when Viola looked in on him to tell him she had a college meeting. She offered to pick up cough mixture on her way back from the city, but he refused anything that was not natural medicine.

'No, no,' he sniffed, 'I will make a ginger and honey tea. I have fresh ginger. I will try that first. Thank you, meu filho. Best wishes with your meeting. Hurry back.'

Viola left the gallery at 9 am and headed to her apartment. She sent a message to Sebastian with a photograph of the note she received to match up with Alonso's artwork.

Martens waited for her in his office.

'Viola, to what do I owe this pleasant visit?'

'Hello Martens. Pleasant? Far from it actually!'

Martens had a permanent frown line between his eyes after decades of courting the burden of legal counsel. When he smiled, the lines between his eyes deepened.

'Yes, yes, I know. And your papa does not know you are seeing me this morning, correct? What happened last night to change our meeting arrangement? I was looking forward to seeing Placido.'

Viola explained her encounter with Alonso, and the note that arrived at her apartment. She told him her neighbors, Garrett, and Janice had moved out without a word.

'Hm... you are going through a lot, my dear. I am so sorry that your Christmas plans are not going as expected. I will hand the note over to the station. It is an important piece to the puzzle regarding the missing artists. I feel sure of that.'

Martens, a man of great virtue, never crossed the law regardless of his client's status in society. Viola trusted him enough to hand over the note should it be required as evidence at some point. A cascade of relief gushed over her that the matter was now in the right hands. This might stop the intruder from persecuting her with unsigned one-line messages dressed in indecipherable expectations.

She left Martens' office at 11:30 am and popped into the greengrocers for lemons and honey and a small bottle of brandy from the adjacent liquor store. This should help her father's recovery from his cold, although he might have a heavy hand with the brandy.

* * *

PLACIDO WAS asleep on the couch when she got back. A quick feel of his forehead confirmed he had a fever. She loosened his clothes and swabbed his forehead with a cool, moist cloth. He opened his eyes and gave her a feeble smile.

'You're back. Have some lunch. Madalena came in and cooked. She is allowed to return, and will come over on Christmas Eve to prepare lunch for us.'

Madalena's delicious beef stroganoff and peach tart was a

godsend to take the edge off her brittle day. But she had no appetite and picked at the meal.

'Papa, you need to eat food that will help you heal faster from this awful cold. Have a generous serving of the beef stroganoff before you drink the ginger and brandy combo?'

'Artista, there's too much in this belly,' he tapped his protruding belly with discontent over his sorry state, 'my taste-buds are dead, I can't enjoy savoring Madalena's cooking. Maybe a small serving later, thank you.'

Placido lapsed into silence, then looked up as though he had a eureka moment.

'Can you believe it is Christmas in two days? Nothing is resolved here. Has your friend arrived from Athens?'

'Don't worry, papa, everything will unfold in its own time. The truth always does. I'm not sure if Matthew has arrived. There's no confirmation from him. I will meet him for drinks on Christmas Eve, and he will join us for Christmas lunch, remember?'

'Good, so he has not changed his mind. He is coming?'

'Yes, he is, what made you think he changed his mind? He might be in Lisbon making his way to Porto as we speak.'

Placido looked through bleary eyes, pressing his temples with both hands, complaining of a throbbing ache between his eyes.

'You need a painkiller papa. This will lower your fever too.'

'Brandy, honey and lemon will do me good, then I should have a nap and be chipper thereafter. Just you wait and see!'

Placido lolled on the couch and was asleep again. Viola went over to the workshop. Nothing was going to stop her from strolling around her father's property. Certainly not Alonso!

Crystal's easel was still up with her partially completed artwork.

Alonso removed his piece from the space.

He did not trust her, and moved his artwork to his cottage. Crystal and her brother were indoors that afternoon, and Viola ventured out to poke around without disturbance.

She meandered around the garden when her cell phone rang putting an end to her quest to snoop around.

It was Matthew letting her know he was arriving in Porto at 7 pm that evening. He wanted to know if she would pop over to see him. She declined, saying her father was nursing a cold and needed pampering. If he was feeling better by morning, she would visit him at his hotel around ten.

By early evening, a red-nosed Placido joined her in the living room.

'Please check if we have everything Madalena requires for Christmas lunch. I need your help with that, meu filho.'

'Yes, certainly. Oh, by the way Matthew and Jungen will be in Porto this evening.'

'Don't hang around here. Go, meet them at the hotel tonight, welcome them to our city.'

'No, Jungen will be exhausted and in need of a good night's sleep, and you are unwell. I want to be here for you.'

'I can look after myself, meu filho. You must welcome them. Please go.'

When she told him she did not want to appear too eager and create a wrong impression, Placido knew, with fatherly insight, that his daughter had already given a part of her heart to this unknown visitor.

Viola prepared gingerbread for Jungen's day at the gallery. Nostalgia kicked in with the memory of Lorenza baking gingerbread early on Christmas morning. The fresh, sweet, spicy aroma was comforting. Deep down she knew Matthew and Jungen would be a welcome distraction for her father's troubled mind.

* * *

Viola got out of bed early and caught the bus into town and walked to the waterway where the Pestana stood majestic in morning light. The sun was out, although there was a chilly freshness in the air. Her stomach dived when she spotted two figures, one adult and the other a child, sitting on the bench near the hotel.

Matthew sensed her arrival, he turned around, eased himself to his feet, and walked to meet her.

'Look who's coming, Jungen, look who's coming!'

Viola felt a flutter and flush upon hearing Matthew's lyrical voice.

The boy bounded towards her.

'Viola-Viola!'

The endearing way in which he said her name made her well-up. There was something about Jungen, from the first time she met him, that made her heart sing.

She swooped him into her arms. He clung to her, giggling and rolling his fingers through her curls.

Matthew watched them with the crinkle around his eyes deepening.

She held out her hand, and he squeezed it. While the ceremonial reunion with Jungen continued, Matthew stood aside as the lad lingered with his head on Viola's shoulder, wanting more cuddles.

'When I told him you were coming to see us this morning, he insisted we wait out here for you. He has missed you.'

Once Jungen had his fill of hugs, he was happy to walk around. Matthew came closer and Viola's pulse ran a marathon around her heart. His husky voice melted her awkwardness.

'It is so good to see you again.'

'Likewise, we need a group hug!'

Viola laughed, afraid her knees would buckle.

Matthew hesitated for a second and then joined in with the child for a Viola hug.

'What a beautiful morning, I expected rain, and what a pleasant surprise to see the city bathed in sunlight.'

'Enjoy it while you can, this is only the second morning that the sun is out since I arrived.'

They headed over to the Pestana for breakfast.

Matthew revealed how tough it was without Bernice.

'I wish I could get a nanny for Jungen tonight, so we can have some alone time.'

Viola's toes curled in her boots. His need for alone time was tempting and unsettling.

'Oh, I hope you don't mind, my father has asked me to invite you over for pre-Christmas dinner and drinks tonight, does that suit you?'

Her knee jerk invitation surprised her and needed approval from Placido.

'I don't mind at all,' he lied, his face telling the story of disappointment, 'it will be great to meet your father. No doubt he is an interesting man.'

Two hours later, Viola left for the gallery with a peck on the cheek from Matthew and a bear hug from the little boy.

She caught herself humming on the bus ride home.

24

Amidst the flurry of Christmas preparations, Viola was uneasy. The situation at Galleria Bardo was still in limbo. Nobody outside of her father, Sebastian and Tempest seemed to care that three artists had disappeared into thin air.

Thoughts of Matthew prodded her already overcrowded mind. Would he be comfortable coming over for dinner tonight, meeting the artists over drinks, and then returning to Christmas lunch tomorrow? He was about to step into her private world for the first time and it scared her. He would be privy to her soul and she was not ready to be transparent with him.

Crystal and the other artists, except Alonso, would join them for drinks after dinner. His last-minute apology came as no surprise to Viola, but it annoyed Placido. Nobody needed a morose, mean-spirited ghost of a person around Christmas. Old Marley, she heard herself mutter, and giggled.

Placido's cold lingered. His fever seesawed, leaving him unusually raggedy during his favorite time of year. He tried to be cheerful.

'I am looking forward to meeting your man tonight, meu filho.'

'He is not my man, papa! It concerns me that you might treat him like he is. He is not anywhere close in that way. Please promise me that you will not create that impression. He is a friend, just a friend!'

'Yes, I get it, I promise not to embarrass you, Artista. Remember when I saw you talking to your classmate at the bus stop when you were in year seven?'

He laughed, coughed, and sneezed in recalling the moment.

'It was not a laughing matter then, nor is it now! Papa, you scared the wits out of poor Timmy, and we were barely thirteen years old. See, I am worried that you will overreact when Matthew arrives.'

'Come on, now, you are an adult, I won't do that again.'

'I hope so.'

'Trust me a little. I will be well-behaved like your students.'

'Now I am worried!'

Madalena was eager to leave as soon as she could to attend to her children. She welcomed Viola's help. Her days at the Bardo household to assist with Christmas preparations made Viola awkward. She detested being served, especially by a less fortunate family member who felt indebted for the financial assistance from her father. Placido loved his cousin and did not expect help with domestic chores. Madalena loved her cousin and the gallery was a refuge from her troubles.

'Will you consider joining us, with the children, for Christmas lunch? We would love your company as our guest, and we have a friend coming over. Papa will be so happy if you joined us.'

'Thank you so much for your kindness. But I cannot accept because I have my ailing father to attend to, and my family is large, that will be more stressful having them outside the home. It is better to be in place where they cannot be a nuisance. I hope you understand.'

'I understand, but it would be lovely to have a full table at Christmas lunch, just like the old days when Lorenza was around.'

Madalena was quiet when Lorenza's name came up. She rarely spoke of how much she missed her baby cousin. With downcast eyes, she whispered the truth of her situation.

'Tomas can't keep off the grog at this time of year and your father will constantly fill his glass. I cannot risk it, you know. You have guests coming to lunch and he will be loud, not to mention an embarrassment to me and the children.'

'You don't have to explain anything to me, I understand. Perhaps you and I can go out to lunch after the new year kicks in.'

'Will you still be here? I really cannot promise anything at this stage. I would love to do that with you. Can we leave it open for now until I know how my father is doing?'

Viola stopped her insistence, and both settled into quiet domesticity, cutting, washing, and cleaning chicken and vegetables.

Then, Madalena asked the awkward question.

'When did you last see your mama?'

'A year ago, it has been a long time. I will call her later this evening to offer my Christmas greetings.'

'I am sure she will be happy to hear from you, that's nice of you. How is she doing these days?'

'Busy. She has a hectic life, teaching and attending dancing classes. Her husband is a competitive dancing champion, so yes, hectic is the right word.'

'I wish I had her courage. It must be wonderful to be care-free. Someday, I hope to go to a dance. It has been years since

Tomas and I had a night out. He would go mental if I suggested taking up dancing lessons!'

Madalena had a hearty laugh imagining her husband's reaction.

Crystal's arrival in the kitchen brought the conversation on Helena and Tomas to a halt.

'Anything I can help with right now?'

'You could help me serve drinks later. That will be the best time for me. Madalena has everything under control for dinner, as usual. Thank you so much for offering to assist. You can never have too many hands when there are guests coming over.'

Crystal agreed and promised to arrive early. Viola watched her leave and wondered if she was brusque in her refusal of help for the meal preparation.

* * *

At 6:30 PM, Matthew and Jungen arrived.

Matthew tried to conceal a bouquet of blood red roses and a ribboned box behind him. Jungen's adoring eyes and obvious joy let out Matthew's secret.

'Viola-Viola, we have caramel fudge for you!'

Matthew turned scarlet and Placido squeezed Viola's arm.

'Ah, I see, the lad knows your fetish for caramel. Perhaps you did not tell him about peanut brittle.'

Viola wished the earth would open and swallow her. Her father was not living up to his promise not to complicate or misconstrue how she felt about Matthew.

She kissed the little lad on both cheeks.

'Do I get a kiss on both cheeks?'

Placido shot Matthew a shocked look, coughed and blamed it on his cold.

'Drinks?' He announced to avoid Viola's glare.

'Yes, please pour a glass for each of us, papa.'

Her father's eyes fell on the roses.

'You should put those in a vase, Artista.'

'These are stunning roses, thank you Matthew. The red complements the mood of the season.'

She smiled at him aware that her father was not missing a beat.

By this stage he was already pouring his second glass of red and the evening had barely begun. He reached out and motioned Jungen to come to him.

'Tell me little one, what do you enjoy about Christmas.'

'Keep the language simple papa, he is still learning English.'

'He has improved since Viola last saw him, so don't worry on that score, Mr Bardo.'

'Placido, please, I don't want the lad thinking I'm past my prime.'

He laughed, clapping his hands, and had the child in a fit of giggles.

Matthew followed Viola to the gallery foyer. She took the flowers to the altar of her beloved aunt Lorenza.

'I'm glad they seem to have clicked already.'

The sparkle in Matthew's deep eyes warmed her. The moment seemed perfect to place the beautiful bouquet at Lorenza's feet.

'She was a special woman, and Christmas was the ultimate celebration of the year for her.'

Matthew had enough years on his shoulders to know it was best to leave that emotional moment right where it belonged — at the feet of Viola's beloved aunt Lorenza.

Dinner was warm and cozy with the four of them relaxing into each other's company. Viola noted that her father continued to drink far more than the food he consumed. When the artists arrived to join them for after-dinner drinks, his speech was slurred, and all he wanted to do was sing an endless string of Christmas carols. The artists left after an hour and Placido announced his exhaustion with a mighty yawn. He stood up and stumbled. Matthew rose to steady him.

'Easy there, would you like me to walk you to your room?'

'Nah, that won't be necessary, gov!'

Placido blew kisses to Viola and Jungen before he wobbled off to his room.

It devastated Viola that this was Matthew's first impression of her beloved papa.

'I am so sorry Matthew. I do not know what came over him tonight. He should not have had so much wine. He is not usually like this.'

Fortunately, the artists left before the tipsy Placido tripped and swayed out the room. Had Alonso been there, he would have made a monumental moment of her papa's disgraceful exit.

'Please don't apologize. It's the season and we are all going to have at least one day where we have more than we should have consumed.'

Viola was unconvinced that Matthew would ever see her father as a proper gentleman deserving respect for the artist, the father, the man he was in her eyes.

Jungen fell asleep on the couch, and Viola excused herself and returned with her favorite red blanket which she lovingly placed over him.

'He adores you. I have never seen him settle so quickly in an unfamiliar environment.'

Matthew's heavy voice made her tense.

'I think the credit goes to my papa. They really had a good time. I had the best childhood with him. He was my best friend in my growing-up years, and still is.'

'Wow! That is a beautiful thing to hear from a daughter

about her father. But I sense that there is something you are holding back from me. Please know you can tell me anything.'

Viola felt the dam ready to burst. Never had she felt this pressure as one who could hold so much for others. She slowly filled him in on the situation at Galleria Bardo and begged for his silence on the matter.

'I would like to assist if you allow me to. I sense your concern that the police are not acting swiftly enough. Let me know, while I am here, and I am prepared to extend my stay if I can help to find answers.'

'Thank you, but I don't know how you can help, to be honest.'

'Something you do not know about me is that I have trained in the military. I have skills to help detect who Mural Man is, and if he has any link to the missing artists. My hip injury is not a deterrent to my physical capabilities.'

Unknown to him she was privy to his life's details. Thanks to Tempest and the kidnapping case around Jungen, she had the rap on the private past of Mr Matthew Soto.

'Perhaps we can talk after Christmas. I want nothing to mar your time here with Jungen.'

'Whatever makes you happy, just say the word.'

'Thank you for being here. I'm ready to put on a pot of coffee, so would you like to join me for a cup?'

Matthew left Galleria Bardo with Jungen late that night, saddened by Viola's predicament, but happy that there was an unspoken growing understanding between them.

She was excited by the nearness of Matthew but thrust aside her need to feel this way. As a child of divorce, she desired a union that outlived disenchantment.

Whether Matthew could offer her the magic she craved in a relationship was not something she counted on.

25

Placido's sleep broke at 6 am. He struggled to get his feet into his slippers before he padded to the kitchen for a glass of water.

His throat was dry, and his head thundered in a relentless ear-splitting boom until the horror of what happened last night retuned. Viola stood at the kitchen sink, looking out at the garden. Would his Artista forgive him for being a drunken lout?

'Coffee, meu filho?'

His voice was low and trembling.

'Papa, you're up. How are you?'

He could not meet her eye, expecting a scolding for his poor behavior. His bounced from heel to toe for an awkward minute.

'Terrible! I am ashamed for embarrassing you last night. Your friend must think me a royal disgrace, and the child... dear God... how will I undo my despicable behavior!'

Viola knew her father's sorry state ran deeper than just too many glasses of wine. He chose not to speak about his troubles and tattered emotions in a situation that threatened his lifestyle. The weight of his burden started to crumble, and hiding it hurt him more.

'Forget it, papa. Please. Matthew and the boy will be here by midday. You need to pull yourself together.'

Placido shook his head.

'How will I ever redeem myself with Matthew and the boy, how?'

'Everybody has their low, Sir Toby Belch moments. You taught me that, papa. Have a shower, freshen up and I promise you will feel heaps better, now let me give you a hug. Merry Christmas, put on that wonderful smile!'

'Dear merciful God! A Toby Belch moment, no!'

'I'm kidding! Get thee to the bathroom!'

She laughed and nudged him towards the door.

He shot her a mournful look.

'I will make it up to you, Artista, I promise.'

Her once sociable father was unhappy, unsure of himself and afraid. She promised herself that her trips to see him would be more frequent than they had been.

* * *

MATTHEW ARRIVED at twelve noon with Jungen in tow, five minutes after Crystal and Dillon came over. Alonso made no appearance.

Jungen rushed to Placido for a hug. His relief was clear in his laughter.

'You two have become bosom buddies! If I am not careful, I might lose my place in Jungen's affection.'

Matthew laughed, hoping that Placido would feel comfortable around him after last night's overindulgence.

'Papa has always had that effect on children. So, you better watch out Matthew! Looks like I might lose my place too!'

Placido chuckled and gave Matthew a friendly handshake.

Viola's inner sigh acknowledged that the day held the promise for merriment.

Crystal served the entrée without being asked. Viola was grateful for her presence.

Conversation and laughter permeated the Bardo gallery home. It had been many years since Placido hosted a Christmas gathering.

Crystal put Viola in a spot.

'Is Matthew your sweetheart?'

Her nervous giggle said more about her heart than she was prepared to admit.

'No, not at all! We met when I worked for him in Athens. I was the boy's English tutor for a brief spell.'

'I thought you worked at a music academy there.'

'I did a stint of moonlighting as a tutor.'

Viola hoped Crystal would never speak to Matthew about how they met in Athens. He knew nothing about her vigilante work. Nobody except her father knew the role she played outside of her teaching, and he respected his daughter's privacy. She had to maintain her credibility with Crystal, who was a vital source of information on Alonso's dark side.

'Please don't mention to Matthew that we spoke about the work I did for him in Athens. He is protective of the boy and a very private man.'

Crystal nodded, but Viola saw her dubious look.

Crystal and Dillon left the party after dessert, to call their family overseas with their Christmas greetings. Placido took Jungen for a walk in the garden giving Matthew space with Viola.

'That was a wonderful lunch, thank you. The first family gathering in a long time for me. The artists are interesting folk, but I felt the underlying tension with what's happened here.'

'Madalena deserves the credit for the scrumptious lunch. I appreciate the artists accepting papa's invitation to drinks last night and lunch today. They have immense respect for him. Papa was nervous and embarrassed about seeing you today after last night. Thank you for easing things for him.'

'You have a wonderful loving father. We all have our vulnerable days when life throws us a challenge. Heaven knows I have had many of those. Before we sidetrack deeper into my most embarrassing moments, we need to discuss how I might assist you with the situation here.'

'I will take your offer, as I know things are volatile and the stranger I keep encountering cannot see me again. But may we please leave the logistics until tomorrow?'

'Anything you say, madam.'

He lowered his head, and reached for her hand, holding it against his chest. He wondered if she was fobbing him off but she surprised him when she leaned forward, overcome by the desire to kiss him. He responded, gently at first, and lingered until they both pulled away when they heard a cough behind them.

'Sorry to disturb you, Ms Bardo. Where might I find your father?'

Alonso hovered at the door with a condescending smirk dancing on his devilish lips. He killed her first intimate moment with Matthew and had the audacity to show up after declining her father's invitation to Christmas lunch.

'He's in the garden, but is not accepting visitors today. Can it wait until tomorrow?'

She would not let him ruin the wonderful Christmas cheer that had descended on their home.

'Yes, it can wait until tomorrow. Enjoy your afternoon, Ms Bardo.'

The hideous smirk returned, followed with a long, hard look at Matthew.

'I never thought that you could ever be brusque. Who is this person with the ability to sharpen your knife?'

'Claws are more like it! Trust me, you do not want to know who he is. I have so many suspicions about him.'

'Act on it then, intuition often holds the truth.'

'He is dark and subversive.'

She stood up and paced the room. Agitation poured from every pore. Intimacy, now cold after Alonso's untimely intrusion.

'You need some air. We should go outside to Placido and Jungen.'

* * *

WHEN THE HOUSE was quiet and settled after all the Christmas guests had left, Tempest requested that Sebastian set up a conference call between the three of them.

Tempest cleared her throat and in her usual husky voice asked Viola what she intended doing to get closure for her father.

'Will you accept Matthew Soto's offer to check on what Mural Man is up to?'

'I am, but cannot tell him too much about my vigilante PI work.'

'What does he know?' Sebastian piped in.

'The nitty-gritty of what he knows and does not know is not a priority, Sebastian,' Tempest hissed.

Tempest silenced Sebastian and shocked Viola with her sudden outburst. He clammed up with no apology.

'He knows enough about my suspicions regarding Mural Man and a bit on Alonso.'

'Let him get into the warehouse tomorrow. I will provide police backup. However, he might not need it with his military prowess. You are not to remain near the site while he is inside the warehouse.'

'Why is that?' Viola asked.

'It is my gut warning me to caution you not to loiter near the warehouse after Matthew goes in.'

Viola knew this was not the time to cross question Tempest. She had chastised Sebastian into a silent corner, and she needed her on this investigation to end her father's problems. Placido was showing signs of falling apart, and swiftness was a necessity with three artists in limbo.

Tempest revealed that she had people tracking Mural Man's movements to establish his connection with Tony.

'Thank you, Tempest. I will get moving on this with Matthew and keep you and Sebastian posted.'

'It's better to keep both your listening devices hooked to us.'

'Consider it done.'

'Stay safe, Viola,' Sebastian whispered.

By 11 pm, with her father sound asleep, Viola slipped out of the gallery and made her way to the Pestana.

At two-thirty am, Placido went to the bathroom and checked in on Viola. He knew she was a nighthawk, pulling an all-nighter in a reading marathon when she had a wonderful book. A strip of light under her door confirmed she was awake. He tapped twice before opening the door.

Her tidy bed did not alarm him. He assumed she was spending the night with Matthew.

'Meu filho, you're in love at last,' he whispered and padded back to his room.

26

———

At 5 am, Viola left Matthew across the street from the warehouse. She turned on her listening device and made her stealthy trek back to the gallery before Placido was ready to greet the day.

She put on a pot of coffee and took a cup over to her father's room.

'Artista! You are up early? Or should I say, you're back soon.'

She ignored his comment, and he knew not to pursue her night-time jaunt.

'What are you doing today, meu filho?'

'Having a quiet father-daughter day, but I forgot to mention that Alonso came over to the house looking for you yesterday afternoon.'

'Oh, what does he want after spurning my lunch invitation?'

'Call him now and find out. Why wait?'

'I will. Did you have a good night?'

He grinned and got no reply.

* * *

PLACIDO FOUND Alonso in the rose garden and caught him off guard with his blunt question.

'What was the urgency that you needed to see me yesterday?'

Alonso turned to Placido with a grave look etched on his unsmiling face.

Placido's lack of tolerance for this theatrical display was obvious in his raised chin and pout.

'I received this note yesterday morning. It was left under my door. I did not want to disturb your lunch, that is why I called at the house in the afternoon.'

He clung to the note.

'So, what does it say? Hand it over if you intend me to know its contents.'

Alonso hesitated, then handed the note to Placido. He read it with widened eyes, sighed, read it again and burst out laughing.

'You know this note is a hoax? It has no signature. Who is the sender? What do they refer to? What is it that they really want?'

Alonso narrowed his eyes.

'Well, they request the delivery of three paintings from Galleria Bardo.'

'Who are *they*, and *what* paintings?'

Alonso's closed his eyes and shook his head.

'Did you read the fine print at the bottom of the note?'

'I can't see fine print without my reading glasses. Tell me, what does it say?'

Alonso exhaled in exasperation, puffed his chest, and snatched the note from Placido.

If this is not delivered in twenty-four hours — Galleria Bardo will burn to the ground!

Alonso's face shone with his misplaced victory over Placido.

'Now what do you say to that?'

'A load of nonsense! That is what I say! No delivery address, no named person making the request, so I will forget about it. The question that begs an answer is how did you come to be the recipient of this anonymous note that targets me, huh?'

'As the messenger, I have done my duty. I brought it to your attention and do not appreciate your insinuation.'

Alonso stomped off.

His biting tone surfaced after a long brewing period. Such an attitude did not happen in the moment.

It was not possible for anyone to enter the gallery grounds undetected with heightened police security in place. In his hurried, angry departure, Alonso dropped the note on the footpath.

Placido had a valuable piece of evidence to hand over to Martens.

Viola waited in her father's office to hear why Alonso was desperate to seek him out on Christmas Day. There was something about him that irritated her from the first day they met, and irritation grew to suspicion with his subsequent random, surreptitious appearances.

Her father marched down the hallway at an unusual speed. Viola rushed to the door to find him panting, strident, mumbling something incoherent.

'Papa! What did Alonso do to upset you this way?'

'Bah! He must think me a fool to believe the rubbish that he just served!'

'I knew he was a sinister piece of work. Whatever it is, you must call Martens and explain that we have suspicions about him.'

Viola knew, with no tangible evidence yet, that Alonso had a hand in the disappearance of the artists. She shivered thinking what else he was capable of, and he was still within the walls of her father's gallery! Placido was Alonso's victim for something unknown to them. The note although poorly constructed harnessed her fears.

* * *

THERE WAS no word from Matthew.

Madalena relieved Jungen's babysitter at the hotel and took him to her home by late afternoon. If Matthew did not return that evening, Viola would take the child to the gallery for the night. How would she explain to her already spooked father why the child was there without his uncle?

A text message to Sebastian confirmed Matthew's silence.

She apologized to Martens for calling so late and disturbing him during the festive break. His candid manner turned into anger when he heard that Matthew Soto was at the warehouse.

'How could you get an outsider involved? Your father's safety is at risk. That is irresponsible of you, Viola! I wish you had consulted with me before you did this.'

'Trust me, I would not put my father's safety at risk. Matthew is highly skilled in military tactics, US Army Special Forces in fact. I trust that he will bring back the information that we seek.'

There was no way she could tell Martens that Tempest and Sebastian were in discussion with her on the way forward with Matthew as the front man. He was upset with her and what was done could not be undone now.

Jungen was fretful, and wanted to go back to the hotel. It was time to bring the boy to the gallery. He was excited when Viola arrived. She had not thought through how she would explain why the boy was spending the night at the gallery.

Matthew's safety was unknown. She got him into this situation, and hoped he was safe. Jungen asked if his *onkel* was at the gallery with her father.

'No sweetheart, your uncle went to a meeting. That is why I'm taking you to spend the night at my house.'

He accepted her answer and asked if she would tell him many stories, and if he could sleep in her room. Viola was grateful there were no tantrums from the boy while she fretted over why there was no word from Matthew.

Placido's jaw dropped when he saw the child. She silenced him with fiery eyes.

'Later, I will explain it all later, papa.'

She raised her eyebrows, warning him not to pursue the matter.

By 9:30 pm Jungen was asleep and Viola went to the gallery office to offer her father an explanation.

'What is going on, Artista? Why is the lad here without his uncle? I feel like I'm caught in the middle of a mystery because nobody is telling me anything!'

'Sorry papa, I should've told you that I might have to watch over Jungen if Matthew was late returning from his meeting today. He'll be back by morning.'

She sincerely hoped he would.

'Look, don't misjudge me, I love having the child here but... but... everything seems so confusing.'

The time had come to give her father a piece of the truth. His anxiety had elevated and she feared his blood pressure was escalating to dangerous level.

'Come papa, come and sit next to me, let me explain something to you.'

She told him that she had enlisted help from Matthew to trace the missing artists. That was all she could reveal. The warehouse, Mural Man, her early morning spying sessions at the warehouse had to remain a secret.

Her father listened, asked her to re-explain why Matthew went out on his own to find the artists. She told him Matthew's military training was needed to investigate while the police were taking some festive down time.

'I am on tenterhooks, Artista. I am expecting another note to turn up any day, threatening me personally, or perhaps threatening you. This is my worst nightmare! I really don't know what to do.'

'Let us wait till morning. I am sure things will look up then.'

'I fear that the lad's uncle is in danger. How can we do this to him?'

He closed his eyes, trying to shut out the confusion.

There was a faint knock on the office door. They looked at each other. It was after eleven.

'Is someone out there at this hour?'

'I'll check, papa.'

Viola walked to the door and cautiously opened it. A white-faced Crystal stared at her with tears streaming down her cheeks.

'Crystal! What's happened? Come in.'

'It's Alonso... Alonso...'

'What has he done now?'

'He's taken, Dillon. He held a gun to his head when he brought him to my room...'

'What! Did you call the policeman on watch duty? Artista call the station and Martens please.'

'No, please, Mr Bardo, I am afraid that if we call the police station, he will shoot Dillon, please don't call the police just yet.'

'How on earth did they get out of the building without the policeman on guard stopping him?'

'I followed them to see where Alonso was taking Dillon and realized that the policeman on watch was not at his post. I fear something might have happened to him too.'

'Dear, dear, God! What is going on?'

'Papa, we must remain calm. We cannot give in to Alonso's ploys. He wants us stressed to the max, hoping we will slip up. Let us keep our heads clear and think about the best way to resolve the situation.'

'What is wrong with you, Artista, a ploy? Crystal's brother has been kidnapped at gunpoint — you call this *a ploy*?'

'Calm down, papa. We need to support Crystal now.'

The enemy, an invited guest within the walls of Galleria Bardo, had made his move!

Matthew reached into his pocket for his phone to send Viola an update. It was not on him.

Gone!

His heart sank. Viola was cut off from listening in to the situation as it evolved in the warehouse. No outside contact left him vulnerable. Things were quiet after Mural Man returned from his bread run. No threat, no need for outside help.

He crawled along the cold concrete floor, feeling his way around, hoping his phone had slid into a corner. Then his heart sank when he saw a thin silver glint beneath the roller door. Unknown to him, his cell phone slipped out of his pocket when he crawled in. The roller door crushed it on its downward slide. The clanging crescendo masked the flattening of his only means of connection with Viola.

An eerie quietness pervaded the warehouse, making it safe for him to venture to the inner door that led to the kitchen. He paid careful attention to how Mural Man opened the door earlier that morning. There was no movement on the other side of the door as he turned the doorknob twice to the right followed by a quick turn to the left.

The door swung open!

He surveyed the ceiling and walls, searching for hidden cameras that might pinpoint his movement. He crawled on all fours across the kitchen floor to the entrance of the open space beyond — the space that Viola said housed artworks in progress. He stepped in and stopped when he saw a woman sitting at an easel with her back to him. She paused when he entered the workspace, sensing a change in the air. Her sensitivity, her intuition, told her that someone was behind her. She turned her head to listen and gasped when she saw Matthew. He placed a silencing finger on his lips and held his palms together to signal he came in peace. The woman nodded, and he motioned for her to move to him. She pointed to her foot. A chain riveted her leg to the concrete floor.

He crept closer and whispered, 'Galleria Bardo.'

She nodded.

They heard footsteps approaching from the passageway to the left of where the woman sat. Matthew slid out of sight behind a room divider into a space with hundreds of paint tins of all sizes and shapes. A long cupboard under the large steel benchtop offered him safety. He crawled into it trying not to wince with the searing pain in his hip, as he stretched to pull the door shut.

He heard a male voice.

'Are you almost done?'

'I need another day, please.'

'I instructed you to have this finished today. The buyer is demanding the release of the painting.'

'I am really sorry... I can't rush this.'

The tension in the woman's voice spelt her fear.

'Voltaire is going to work in here this evening. I expect you both to paint side-by-side with no conversation between you. Do I make myself clear?'

'Understood.'

'I do not want a repetition of what happened on Sunday. No conversations between the artists! Simple instruction! I will come in often to ensure that you both are working every second of the time I give you. I will be back.'

Matthew figured that the woman was Ariel, and the male voice confirmed that Voltaire was on site. Viola needed this information. Lamar had to be somewhere in the building.

A slow heavy-footed gait, followed by the clanging sound of metal dragged on ground, emerged from a passageway behind Matthew. Mural Man and Voltaire walked into the workspace. When he heard the lock click, he crawled out the cupboard and peered around the wall divider.

Ariel caught a glimpse of him, from the corner of her eye, and shook her head without looking at him. He pulled back.

'I want both pieces finished before sunrise. We are under pressure to get the shipment out. I have too much at risk and cannot have you both wasting your time in idle chitchat. Get on with it now and I will be back.'

The male voice Matthew heard, next, was guttural.

'Art takes time. It has a mind and mission of its own. I don't suppose you ever heard of the muse that guides the hand of the artist?'

Matthew sucked in his breath when the sound of something crashing against the wall shook the room, the paint tins rattled, threatening to topple over.

Mural Man flung a chair across the room.

'Do not give me your cheek. You are nothing here! You are under my command and I have a lot to lose if you do not finish these paintings by morning. Get it done! Or your safety is at risk.'

'Ah, a threat! I can't wait to tell the police what has been going on here.'

'Voltaire! Please... stop... please...'

Ariel's amplified distress suggested that Mural Man was aggressive enough to harm them.

Matthew had to let Viola know that tension was escalating inside the warehouse. Police had to be informed that the artists were alive.

With no communication, he was helpless.

VIOLA SETTLED Crystal and left her in Placido's care while she called Sebastian.

Neither Tempest nor Sebastian had heard anything from Matthew. His safety had been compromised. He needed police back-up. They promised him protection. Viola accepted full responsibility for failing him.

Tempest was the only optimistic person among the three, believing in Matthew's ability to overcome any situation he faced.

'I can't send the police in just yet. This is the only opportunity we have for Matthew to find out what is going on inside the warehouse. I have a suggestion, although I hesitate to recommend it. You should go to the warehouse to check out the situation, but only from the outside. You should not venture inside. We cannot have you and Matthew out of listening range.'

Sebastian was quiet during this discussion until he decided it was time to say what Viola had left out of her update.

'Alonso has proven to be a scoundrel. He is on the run with Crystal's brother, it is imperative that you send the troops in now.'

Tempest listened, mulled over the course of action.

'I will give it an hour for you to get there to let us know what's happening to ensure that sending in the police is the right thing to do.'

'Without further ado, and with due respect, I believe we are wasting time talking, I should get there now.'

'Agreed,' Tempest and Sebastian sung in unison.

'Make sure you turn on your device from the minute you head out.'

* * *

Viola said a silent prayer and headed to her father's office. She could not divulge what was going on at the warehouse. All she said was that she had to go down to the police station to explain that Matthew was assisting on the case.

'I cannot believe I'm hearing you say this, Artista. You who has not a shred of trust or belief in the police.'

'Trust me on this, papa. You keep Crystal company and I'll be back soon.'

Crystal's swollen eyes, now slits with the puffiness around them, nodded like a helpless child.

'Please take care of yourself, I intend to find Dillon and bring him back.'

Crystal sunk into the chair, ready to burst into tears again.

Two heart beats claimed Viola, one for her father, and the other for Matthew. She was going to bring them through this.

Donned in her night roaming gear, she grabbed a cab to the city center.

Along the waterway, close to the Pestana, she got off the

195

cab, and sprinted to the warehouse. She had to figure out whether the police should be summoned. Her winged feet ran the race of her life, determined to get there to save three artists and the man whose life was at her mercy. At the corner of the warehouse street she slowed her pace when she saw the ominous building.

Halfway down the street she heard gunfire — three shots in rapid succession.

She fell to her knees, jumped up, and fled behind the building across the street, expecting stray bullets to come flying at her. With every nerve electrifying her body, she was unsure whether the police had got there before her. Then she heard the wail of police sirens deafening the aftermath of gunfire. Four police vehicles sped down the street before grinding to a halt in front of the warehouse.

The door was open! She rushed across, calling out at the top of her lungs.

'Matthew! Matthew! Are you in there?'

An arm yanked her away and snapped handcuffs onto her wrists.

A familiar voice behind her called out.

'Remove the cuffs. She is from Galleria Bardo, this is Bardo's daughter.'

Officer Manning came to her rescue.

She was directed to sit in a police vehicle to wait for further instructions.

As police entered the building a woman dashed out, followed by two men. They had to be the artists because Matthew was not one among them. All three were handcuffed and escorted to another police vehicle. Viola struggled to breathe. Petrified. There was no sign of Matthew. Her eyes searched through dim light, her blurred vision making it diffi-cult to discern the activity at the warehouse entrance.

Had Matthew taken a bullet? Was he injured or heaven forbid, dead!

2 8

A host of scenarios ran through Viola's mind on how to explain what had happened to Matthew to a little lad who adored his *onkel* Matt. Spinning blue and red lights made her queasy. She sat alone, forgotten, in the police vehicle. Nobody came to her with updates on what was going on inside the building.

Matthew lying in a pool of blood is all she could process.

She swallowed back tears on the verge of erupting after weeks of suppressing her emotions.

If he was dead, the blame rested with her decision to send him into an unprotected zone. There was no way she would let Tempest shoulder the blame.

After forty minutes of tormented waiting, she heard a tap on the hood of the police vehicle. The rotating lights hypnotized her reactions as she slipped deep into the safety of mindlessness.

She heard a soft voice which she imagined was Matthew's.

'Open the door, Viola.'

She was numb, and convinced the voice was in her confused head.

The tapping moved to the left passenger window.

She stared, startled.

The outline of a male figure scared her until she registered that Matthew was looking at her.

'Matthew?'

She opened the door, unsure if this was really him.

Her emotions burst like a pent up avalanche. She sobbed into her hands, shaking her head in disbelief.

'I thought they shot you, I imagined you lying on the cold warehouse floor — dead. It killed me thinking how I was going to tell Jungen what had happened to you.'

She reached out to touch his arm, to convince herself that he was not an apparition.

'Hush now. All is going to be fine. Breathe, you have had too much to deal with in recent weeks. Step out the vehicle, let me hug you. You need it.'

Her limp body fell against him. All reserve melted in a fresh wave of tears as she sobbed into his chest, tightening her grip around him until she heard him wince.

'What's wrong?'

She pulled away.

'A bullet grazed my back. The paramedic who arrived with the police attended to it. I will live, never fear!'

'Please do not joke about this. It has been a living nightmare from the moment I heard the gunshots going off inside the building.'

He put his arms around her and twirled her hair around his fingers.

'I am so sorry Matthew. I did not expect you would be injured. This is all my fault.'

'Don't be silly. This could have happened anywhere,

perhaps while I was with Jungen. Thank God he is safe! It's just a bullet graze, and I will be good as new in a few days.'

His soothing voice had her clinging to him, afraid to let him go.

'We should leave now. I will tell you what transpired inside that dreadful warehouse on our way to the gallery. I'll be back in a second, I'm going to look for the investigating officer to tell him that we are leaving the site.'

'I don't think he will allow us to leave. Everybody is inside. Who will you ask? Nobody cares about us in all of this.'

Matthew pointed to the warehouse.

'Look, look who is being taken out in handcuffs to the paddy wagon.'

'Is that Alonso? I had no idea he was inside the warehouse.'

'That's him for sure! The scoundrel! He was the shooter. He had a young man with him, and shot the poor guy. Got him in the hip. '

'Dear God, Crystal's brother, Dillon!'

'Ah! That is why he was familiar. I saw him at Christmas lunch. Poor fellow looked terrified before he went down.'

'Is he gravely injured?'

'He was conscious and talking to the paramedic when I left. But the other man looks like he took a bullet in his chest because he hit the ground hard.'

'Mural Man? It must be him, oh no! I hope he's not dead.'

'I believe it is him from the way you described him.'

'Was anyone else injured when the three shots were fired?'

The wail of two approaching ambulances swallowed her question, but Matthew was quick to respond.

'It will relieve you to know that the three artists are safe. Police have taken them to the station for their statements. So, we will know what happened and why it happened, soon. There goes Crystal's brother and the man you call Mural Man.'

Viola saw two stretcher beds being carried out to the waiting ambulances.

'I have to find out which hospital they are going to. I need the information to pass on to Crystal. She expects me to bring Dillion back, or have news on where Alonso took her brother.'

* * *

AN HOUR later Viola and Matthew sat in the waiting room at General Hospital. Officer Manning arrived soon after for an update.

'Any news on how the two are doing?'

'Nobody will give us any information because we are not next of kin. Perhaps you might have some luck in your uniform.'

Manning marched off to the front desk and was back in five minutes.

'The young man with a bullet in the hip is doing fine, but his next of kin has to be located for information on whether he has any health risks before they proceed with removing the bullet. The removal must be within twenty-four hours before infection sets in.'

'What about Mural Man? Is he going to be okay?'

Officer Manning looked at Viola puzzled.

'Do you know the man? Is that his name?'

Viola's cheeks burned.

'Oh no, I don't know him. He is a familiar sight around the street art in the city. I have seen him a few times at the murals in the lane we both frequented. But I do not know him, it's just a nickname I attached to him.'

Officer Manning nodded. As a man with four teenage daughters, he knew their idiosyncrasies of attaching names to strange things that attracted them.

'Sorry Ms Bardo, but he didn't pull through. Staff were ordered not to divulge anything to the public. Now we have a murder on our hands.'

Viola could not contain her shock.

'Mural Man, gone, I can't believe it.'

She will never know who he was, or why his eyes were familiar.

* * *

It was 4 am when Viola and Matthew got back to Galleria Bardo. She gave Matthew a blanket and a pillow and told him to grab two hours shut eye on the lounge room couch. Jungen was asleep on her bed, she would snatch some sleep on the chair at the foot of the bed. She had to be fresh for the day ahead. Thoughts on how Matthew was allowed to leave the crime scene, although technically he was an intruder in the warehouse, left her sleepless.

Could Tempest have worked her magic on that?

Like clockwork, Placido pottered around at 6 am. He dashed to Viola when she entered the kitchen and held her close.

'Meu filho! What has happened? You are as white as a sheet. Is Matthew back?

'Much has happened, papa. Yes, Matthew is back, but I have to speak to Crystal to let her know that Dillion took a bullet in the skirmish.'

'What?'

'We have to keep calm, please, papa. Dillon is not dead. He took a bullet in the hip and Crystal is needed at the hospital this morning to confirm whether he has any health risks before they remove the bullet.'

'I will come with you to see Crystal. Poor lady, she was beside herself last night after you left, worrying about your safety.'

'Oh dear, I hope she's going to handle this news we are about to give her.'

'Are the artists safe? Have they been found?'

In the hype of everything, Viola forgot to set her father's mind at ease over what had troubled him for many weeks.

'Yes, papa, they are alive and well, thank God. But they are in police custody making their statements and God knows what else they are being asked to do. I am not happy with them being taken to the station so soon for a debriefing. They have endured much.'

Placido raised his palms to the heavens.

'But, thank God they are alive!'

The events overnight exhausted Crystal. She had dark circles under her eyes and looked like she needed a sedative. Viola's update on Dillon fueled her hope that he would be back to his normal self soon.

Crystal spent the day waiting at the hospital until her brother was out of surgery.

Viola headed to her apartment to call Tempest and Sebastian.

'It is sad that Mural Man died in the gunfire last night. Alonso will face the ultimate sentence for this. But the truth must prevail. I have one piece of information that might be helpful to you.'

'What is it?'

Sebastian's curiosity got the better of him.

'Here's the thing, Mural Man, was a Mozambican national. His name is Eka Gimo. That is all I have at this stage.'

'Mozambican? That is an interesting piece of information that I was not expecting to hear.'

Viola's mind darted back to the first day she met him. The haunting familiar eyes, but she could not place why she knew them. Was it because of his nationality that she felt a sense of empathy and camaraderie with him, a man she did not know by name? A stranger, a wayfarer who appeared during her treks in the city. A night walker and before sunrise presence on the street now had a name.

'I expect to bring you more information later today. Sit with that for now and let us see how we can tie up the loose ends. The rest in relation to Alonso is in the hands of the police.'

Viola thanked Tempest and Sebastian, grabbed some items of clothing, and called a cab to get back to the gallery.

She scanned the park across the street from her apartment as she waited for her ride to arrive.

There was no long-cloaked, bearded man hurrying away.

Will she ever know who her Mural Man truly was?

There was much to be grateful for. Crystal confirmed that Dillon's surgery went well. He was in recovery. All his vital signs were good. The three missing artists were safe.

The cloud of suspicion lifted off Galleria Bardo. She hoped this was the end to her father's worries.

Unanswered questions still hung in the air over Mural Man and his fascination with the laneway murals.

The past has a way of intersecting with the present in ways one never imagines possible. Moving on is assured, but the seeds of time remain, springing up in fresh shoots from the soil of challenge.

VIOLA ASKED Matthew to excuse her for a few hours while she had a private conversation with her father.

The gracious Matthew said he would return to the Pestana and call her tomorrow. He understood that the few hours might be a day for the two of them to come to terms with everything that emerged in last forty-eight hours.

She hugged them both at the gallery door. Jungen clung to her for a second, then pulled away, jumping up and down with joy.

'See you later, Viola-Viola!'

He was a happy child, happier than he was in Athens.

'And where did that phrase come from?'

Matthew enjoyed the effect Viola had on Jungen.

'Drumroll! We have an Aussie boy among us!'

'He's a fast learner, just like his uncle Matt.'

'This happens when you leave me alone with him, I teach him my ways.'

Matthew pulled her close and whispered in her ear.

'I hope all goes well with your father today. Call me, please, any time.'

'Thank you, thank you for everything, for being here.'

'See you later, Ms Bardo.'

Matthew grinned as he climbed into the cab with Jungen.

Viola stood at the door a while longer, waving them off, her heart heavy with the overload of information from Officer Manning and Tempest.

Some missing pieces were yet to be linked.

Placido and Viola had the gallery to themselves, the entire place. Crystal and Dillon were at the hospital. The remaining artists were allowed to leave provided they did not leave Porto while the investigation was underway. Lamar, Ariel, and Voltaire were in a safe house at a secret location. Alonso was where he belonged — behind bars.

On the surface all seemed well, but Viola needed to have this conversation with her father.

Placido was in the lounge room tapping on the piano to the tune of *Auld Lang Syne* that he played to perfection. Viola listened at the doorway, losing herself in the melody. She walked in and hugged him from behind.

'You play it so well, papa. You take me back in time with that piece. I have missed playing the piano ever since I got here.

My college post does not allow the flexibility to teach anything remotely musical.'

'Come, sit next to me, let us play a piece together like the old days.'

'Later, papa. I have something to tell you. Matthew and Jungen have returned to the Pestana tonight. It is just you and I and Galleria Bardo! Like old times!'

'What has happened? Why did Matthew and the boy leave?'

'They will be back tomorrow. I have some information to share with you.'

'Matthew is a good sort, I sense it, meu filho,' he smiled, 'is it Dillon? Please don't tell me something has happened to him since we last spoke.'

'No, Dillon is fine, just the way he was when I spoke to you earlier.'

'It seems like I might need a brandy. I sense you have a weighty subject to share.'

'No papa! I need you to be fully alert to what I am going to say. No alcohol, please.'

'Artista, you are right. But one quick question, is this about your mother?'

'Now, where did that come from? This has nothing to do with her.'

'Phew! Go on. I promise not to interrupt.'

They moved over to the couch.

With her hand on her father's shoulder, she told him all she could divulge on Mural Man. His name, Eka Gimo, her suspicion that he might have been the intruder in her apartment block. How he got in past the security and the strange erasure of the surveillance footage gushed out as all she had concealed from him. When she said that Mural Man was a Mozambican national, Placido raised his hand to say something. She continued that she suspected that he placed the note in her letterbox.

'You said, Gimo. Elio's last name. You were too young to know that then.'

Viola absorbed this like a woodpecker in a desert drought. 'Elio was a *Gimo*?'

'Perhaps they are relatives.'

'You know what this means, papa. Somehow, you, or Galleria Bardo, have been the target in this crime. Our worst fear! Hence I was being stalked by the stranger we now know as Eka Gimo.'

'Why?'

'Did you have any communication with Elio's family after his murder?'

'No, I have had no communication ever with his family. It was just him until the news that he was killed, which I read in a newspaper two weeks after his death.'

His eyes, Mural Man's eyes. The familiarity she first saw was all beginning to make sense. Those eyes extracted an empathy she could not explain. Sad eyes above his long wavy beard. He had Elio's eyes! Brothers!

Then her father shared a revealing piece of information.

'I recall receiving a letter a year ago from someone who signed off with the same surname, no first name included. I stashed it inside my desk drawer and never gave it a thought again. Come, let us go over to the office, you can have a look at it.'

Viola paused at Lorenza's portrait and asked for guidance to the truth.

Placido searched through his desk drawer and pulled out a brown envelope. When he unfolded the letter and handed it to Viola, she gasped.

'What is it? Did I miss something in the letter?'

The note was in the same hand as the note on the laneway mural, and the note she received at her apartment.

She read the letter to her father.

You do not know me, but I know you. You help people in need. I am in need, kind sir. My family is in desperate need. Please help me reunite with my loved ones.

Signed, E. Gimo. No first name attached.

The address was a post office box number in Porto. Viola looked at the envelope for the postmark that confirmed the place of origin.

'Papa, did you check this out for who was behind it? This scribe is the same man. All my suspicions are proving true, but the dead don't talk, so we shall never know what he really wanted from either of us.'

'That scoundrel Alonso must have the answers! Soon we shall know the truth. I thought the letter was a hoax, that someone was trying to trick me for money. The name E. Gimo made me think so, given that I helped Elio all those years ago. I put the letter aside and forgot about it until now.'

This revelation jolted the pattern emerging.

'Yes, a hundred percent! The whole thing points to Alonso's connection with Eka Gimo in this, for some unknown reason. Alonso is the kingpin. His name on the artwork was in the same hand. Could Eka Gimo have signed it for him?'

'Why would they want to pull me down, Artista? I am already down. I have nothing to give or lose.'

'Your skills papa and your beautiful artworks, that is what they were after. Please never say you are down, because you are not! You are the greatest artist the world has seen.'

'Oh, my sweet child! I once was, I no longer am.'

'Art never loses value, regardless of the time of creation, as it passes through generations. You are eternal in my heart, papa.'

Placido reached over and hugged his daughter with the last shred of energy he had left. Viola, his Artista, was his inspiration during those trying years. She kept him from falling apart. When everything failed, his Viola was there, a shining light, egging him on, celebrating his passion. His daughter was all the daughters he ever needed.

She understood, that after years of being exploited by money grabbers, he had come to the stage in his life where he pulled back from such demands.

The plea in the letter held her attention.

My family is in desperate need. Please help me reunite with my loved ones.

The larger laneway mural depicted a scared boy hidden in the background, and in the forefront, the salient image of a woman loomed. Her eyes sad, looking at some unpainted entity. Was this the depiction of Mural Man's family?

She found it hard to focus and picked up her phone to look at the murals she photographed. Now that its meaning was unfolding, her heart grew heavy.

'Perhaps if I responded to that letter, gave the man whatever he wanted, I would not be in this pickle today and you would not have got caught in this mess.'

'He would have continued to fleece you. Once given, easily got, they never stop. You can hand this to Martens and get him to do a check for you.'

'Whatever for? The man is dead.'

'I am being selfish in saying that because I am keen to know if Eka Gimo had a family, and whether they are alive.'

'For that reason, I will hand it over to Martens for you to put this to rest.'

'Thank you, papa.'

They made a pot of tea and sat down together at the piano

and played a few old familiar tunes that took her back to the Mozambique she once loved.

Father and daughter had many unresolved thoughts that deterred peaceful sleep.

Viola picked up her phone to message Matthew and found an email notification waiting for her.

Rob Dwyer, her Blackwater headmaster, sent her his best wishes for the festive season, but it was his appeal below his cheery greeting that unsettled her.

He was having a surgical procedure at the end of January and asked if she could return to Blackwater Performing Arts Academy to take his place as acting principal!

How on earth was she going to sit in his chair when some staff members were already eyeing the seat, and she barely spent more than a term there in recent years?

His reply would have to wait until tomorrow. She had to give it careful thought and perhaps run it by Matthew, who was sure to give her his rational opinion. Her father's emotional response would be, *just take it, Artista, take it, Rob Dwyer knows your worth!*

She rolled over and fell asleep when the sun peeped in through her bedroom blinds.

3 0

Officer Manning asked Viola to come down to the station to provide her statement on the happenings at Galleria Bardo and the shooting at the warehouse.

She replayed the sequence of events many times from the first day she arrived at her father's gallery to the night Mural Man was shot. This would be an unemotional, verbatim statement.

It was not until she described her encounters with Mural Man that she felt an emptiness. It was time to drop the nickname and refer to him as Eka Gimo. The name somehow alienated the empathy his eyes drew. But it was impossible to view him as a villain in Alonso's schemes.

For a large commanding station, the meeting room was a pokey, miserable, inhospitable place. The bare cement floor was no different to that of Mural Man's warehouse where his life came to a tragic end. A ray of sunlight forced its way through the tiny, ceiling-high, barred window, casting a shadowed halo above her head. The suffocating space made her uncomfortable. Manning's effort to uphold a cheerful countenance did nothing to ease the tension.

The commanding officer recorded everything Viola said regarding Mural Man, but she avoided revealing the conversation she had with her father on the letter and their speculations on who E. Gimo might be. Marten's looked into that side of things for them.

She could not subject her father to more questions on issues that brought guilt to the fore for not reaching out to Eka. The letter was safely in Martens' hands to avoid being cross questioned for keeping it a secret. A secret he did not intend. It was a request he had the right to ignore. Placido did not want hangers-on with hard-luck stories in his now quiet life.

When she asked what Alonso's involvement was, the commanding officer told her everything she needed to know to clarify what she witnessed in the weeks leading up to the catastrophic night at the warehouse.

Alonso was the right-hand man to a larger underground extortion organization. They preyed on artists who had a flourishing career, were close to retirement, or breaking their way into the artistic world. He was the point of contact inside Galleria Bardo to have Lamar, Voltaire and Ariel taken. The officer handed her a summation of the artists' statements on their experience after the abductions.

All three cited Alonso's betrayal of their trust. He led each one of them outside on each of the three nights. They recalled being blindfolded and taken to a car that brought them to the warehouse. The unknown driver handed them over to a nasty old man. They believed that the unseen driver was part of the syndicate. He was silent throughout the journey to the drop off point where he handed them over. Ariel made a note that the old man was violent and prone to sudden outbursts of anger. He beat her on the head with a heavy frying pan when she complained of exhaustion or having cramps in her fingers. The artists painted for sixteen hours a day with one break of fifteen minutes for lunch. This imposed production line did not consider that they had human needs, and that fatigue was inevitable. When Viola read Ariel's comment, it heartened her that the man in the long, striped coat was considered kinder than the older man. Her gut was not wrong on the soul of the man she saw mesmerized by the laneway street art.

Voltaire noted the high level of anxiety in the man with the long, striped coat. He repeatedly told them that he had a lot at stake, and if they knew what was good for them, they would get the paintings done as instructed. He also asked Voltaire to assist with packing the completed paintings into large cardboard boxes taken from the warehouse floor. Viola had a flashback of crouching behind the towering corrugated cardboard boxes. At that point she had no idea that this was a hothouse production line that abused artists under treacherous conditions. Large shipments of paintings went to wealthy overseas buyers. Never in her wildest dreams did she imagine that in the abandoned warehouse a hive of activity churned in the hidden back room.

Lamar complained about being locked in a tiny cell-like room with no food or water for two days when he threw down his paintbrushes, protesting doing more than was humanly possible. They did not see Alonso again until the night of the shooting.

The artists concurred that an argument broke out between the man in the long, striped coat and Alonso when he asked for his pay. Alonso's retort was that Mural Man would never see his family again, so he had to keep working if he valued his life. It was then that the man lunged at him and both tussled on the ground until two shots rang out, one hitting Dillon in the hip, the other grazing Matthew on his back when he attempted to intervene. The third shot, the fatal shot, struck Mural Man in the chest.

The description of the bloody scene unnerved Viola. Mural Man's haunting familiar eyes clung in her memory. Unknown to Viola and Matthew, he was dead upon arrival at ER.

Viola looked the commanding officer in the eye, leaning forward over the broken wooden table.

'Why were we not told that Mur... the man was dead? Officer Manning asked, and he was told he had died. Why this subterfuge?'

The officer cleared his throat, thrown by the mild-mannered Viola's sudden anger. He pulled back in his seat.

'Hospital staff were under strict instruction not to divulge anything to the public as the crime had just occurred and we had no statements at that point. We had to determine the man's involvement in the abductions from your father's gallery and whether his death would have further ramifications.'

Viola stilled her emotions and accepted that crucial information had to be private until after the investigation had started.

A shadow fell over the commanding officer's face. He pulled his seat closer to the table.

'Sadly, very sadly, Ms Bardo, nobody came forward to identify nor claim the man. The ugly side of what we face in the work we do. Or should I say the ugly side of life?'

Viola eyes prickled, but she had no intention of letting the commanding officer know that she felt a deep, strange connection to Mural Man.

'That is as much as we have from the artists and a further piece of information on the driver is that he is a young man known to be Alonso's first cousin, a man only known as Tony from Caracas.'

Viola shuddered as an uncontrollable twitch claimed both her legs. Tony! He asked many personal questions about Galleria Bardo and tried to get close to her. She did not let on that Tony was her student, or that she saw him in conversation with Mural Man in the laneway. She asked how he was found.

'He came forward and revealed his identity. Mostly, he is innocent, acting as a driver, or go-between for Alonso. His sentence will be a light one, perhaps community service is the most he will receive. Once he heard that Alonso was in custody he panicked and came forward without being asked to. If he did not give him self up, we would not have known that he drove the artists from the gallery to the warehouse.'

'Quite a tangle! Alonso had many people on his payroll.'

'Yes, he is undoubtedly the arch villain in this. He will remain behind bars for as long as I can persuade the judge to hold him — for life. You are free to leave the country whenever you choose, as is your father. The ban on your movements should not have happened. On behalf of the station, I apologize for the strain this caused your father.'

Viola looked up at the commanding officer, softened by the decency of his apology. She thanked him, wished officer Manning a pleasant day and walked out of the dingy meeting room into a sunlit morning.

Forty-eight hours later, Martens arrived at the gallery.

What he revealed ripped Viola's heart to shreds in her agreement with the commanding officer's assessment of, *the ugly side of life.*

Two and a half years ago, Mural Man's wife and son disappeared from Maputo after a day out shopping. She was a skilled potter and painter who shipped her wares to Paris, Milan, Greece, and New York. Her pottery and paintings received rave reviews internationally. Mural Man worked with her in their family business. When Elio was murdered, Eka Gimo got caught in the gunfire outside their home. His injured leg caused the permanent lopsided gait that Viola grew to know so well. After Elio's brutal death, Eka slipped into ongoing bouts of depression. He named his son in memory of his brother. Mural Man's wife forged a connection online with the extortion organization linked to Alonso. He struck up a relationship with her and came to Mozambique and took her and her son to Lisbon.

Martens traced her movements there. She went to Britain a week after her arrival in Lisbon and placed her son in an elite private boarding school.

Viola cringed at the advantage she gave the child, but denied him a family life and the chance of ever seeing his father again. All to fulfill her own needs.

Cruel, cruel fate of the man in the long, striped coat with his lopsided gait. He never saw his wife, or boy again. Her work continued to flood the international market, taunting him with her ghostly presence after she left him alone and penniless. He could not afford private investigators to find her, and the police turned a deaf ear to his pleas, citing her disappearance as a runaway wife. Mural Man lived in the hope that she would return to him with their son.

Alonso played on his vulnerability and used him as his mule.

Mural Man was in Porto and his wife, unknown to him, was so close, in Lisbon. She shacked up with Alonso in a remote location and had a baby girl. Viola unashamedly wept for Mural Man's loss, but was glad he did not know of his wife's love affair with Alonso.

Martens and her father gave her the space to work through her emotions.

'My Artista has always been a soul for others. She feels Eka Gimo's pain like it is her own.'

'Your daughter is in your image, my friend. You artists lead emotional lives. The world is a better place because of you.'

'I apologize for my tears, but had you seen him transfixed by those paintings, and then to know his sorrow, it rips your heart out.'

Both gray beards nodded their understanding.

'And,' Martens continued, 'your neighbor at the apartment was on Alonso's payroll. All the missing pieces now fit on how the note came to your door.'

'I had my suspicions when the contusion on Garrett's neck vanished, and when he left without saying goodbye after pretending to care about my safety.'

Once she was alone in her room, Viola replied to Rob Dwyer's email. He needed her and deserved an answer.

My dearest Mr Dwyer,

You will always be Mr Dwyer to me! I am saddened to hear that you have been unwell. I will return to Sydney at the start of the new term but cannot promise to take on the acting principal position. We can talk early in the new year.

Until then, take great care.

Viola

Rob teased her about her formality of address. Her respect for him was that of a student to her teacher. That was sacred, never trivialized.

Soliciting Matthew's thoughts on whether she should accept Rob's offer were squashed. This was urgent. Rob Dwyer's call for help could not go unnoticed.

Now she had to let Vanessa Smythe and Howard know that she was withdrawing her contract with the college. And then there was her father...

Such was life's lessons when the pain of others shoots an indelible arrow through the heart.

31

Ariel moved into the artist's accommodation after speaking to Placido about taking up residence there, once she knew what she was doing with her life. He refused to take rent money from her and told her she could stay on until the end of January and then decide if she wanted to become a permanent tenant. Lamar and Voltaire left with the promise to keep in touch and visit whenever they were in the country.

It was New Year's Eve, and the dark veil had lifted off Galleria Bardo.

While universal resolutions were being planted for the forthcoming year, Viola had an announcement to make to two men, one the center of her world, the other who put his life on the line for her father.

Placido was reading in the garden.

'Lovely to see you so relaxed this morning.'

'Perhaps it is, indeed, all's well that ends well, although the sadness of Eka's life and death still hangs over us. How are you feeling this morning, meu filho?'

'I am okay, thank you. May I steal a few minutes of your precious reading time? I have something to share.'

Placido's book slammed shut. He sat upright in the garden deck chair.

'What is it, Artista? I get worried when you want to make a formal announcement.'

'Well, it's not as serious as what we've experienced of late. But Rob Dwyer is unwell and needs surgery and has asked if I would return to Blackwater Ridge to assist him in his duties for term one.'

Placido listened to Viola with a concerned frown.

'I am sorry to hear Rob is unwell. Yes, you must return to help him. He does much for you by allowing you to come and go as you do. Go with my blessing.'

Viola hugged her father with all her might.

'Oh papa! You have made this so easy. Thank you. If only you could have been my mother too! She would have given me an earful. Thank you for being so understanding.'

'My dear Artista, no two parents will ever be the same. We are yin and yang. Do not be too hard on your mother. She has been quiet with no Christmas message from her, and we neglected to send her a message with all the troubles going on here.'

'The latest news of what happened in Porto has not hit the international media yet, or she would have called us or rather me to check if you were okay. She still cares about your wellbeing.'

Placido's eyes lit up, 'Do you really think she cares?'

'I do. I will call her with our New Year greetings tomorrow.'

'Good, she will be happy to hear from you.'

Viola told Placido of her plan to move her things out of the apartment to spend the month at the gallery before she headed back to Australia.

'When do you plan to return?'

'I will leave in the last week of January. Blackwater Ridge Academy opens in the first week of February.'

'It will be literally off the plane and into the classroom for you.'

Just as Viola predicted, Placido was ecstatic that Rob expected her to hold the fort for him as acting principal.

'That is a great opportunity, take it. Rob knows you can do it.'

The politics she might face was not something her father needed to know.

Then he asked, trying not to seem inquisitive about her private life.

'Have you spoken to Matthew about your plans?'

'I will when he comes over for dinner tonight. I am cooking today. I gave Madalena the weekend off from caring for us.'

'Sounds like you have it all worked out. Pardon me for saying what you already know, but Matthew is gaga over you. Surely you know that. Can't take his eyes off you!'

'Gaga? Papa that is so funny!'

She held her belly and laughed so hard, something she had not done in weeks.

After a beautiful hour and a half together, Viola prepared dinner. Apple pie for dessert was both her father's and Jungen's favorite.

She went over to Ariel's cottage to invite her to dinner. With Crystal gone, she did not expect any help in the kitchen from Ariel. She was an other worldly soul, not quite present with what went on around her, but a gentle spirit that Jungen would enjoy.

* * *

AFTER DINNER, Viola tapped on the piano over a glass of wine in the warm company of her father and Matthew. Ariel exhausted Jungen with her outdoor activities and soon he was sound asleep.

Placido and Ariel excused themselves for the night and exchanged best wishes for the New Year.

Viola moved over to the couch with her fingers entwined.

'That looks serious.'

'Yeah, I have some news, but I'm not sure whether it's serious or the right time to let you know.'

Matthew bent forward with raised eyebrows.

'Out with it then. I don't like it when I get only a hint of information.'

She enjoyed how comfortable he was around her and Placido.

'Oh, that sounds like a military threat! But on a truthful note, I am returning to Australia earlier than expected. By the end of January, three and a half weeks to go, and I shall be back at my old school, or rather my home school.'

'What's prompted the change to your original plan of spending three months here?'

Matthew was a good listener, never interrupting her like her father did, even when eager to know more. His crinkled brow conveyed his confusion.

She explained that she did not want to take on the acting principal position while Rob was on sick leave. He questioned her and understood her discomfort in assuming the role even though it was brief stint. His response was not what she expected. He did not express disappointment that she was leaving when he planned to extend his stay in Portugal. Her reasons were private, and he would never tread on her dreams.

She imagined he would ask her not to leave, and was disappointed with his placid, respectful acceptance of her plans.

* * *

VIOLA CALLED her mother in Cape Town and wished her and her husband the best for the new year. Helena was happy she called, and made a feeble excuse about not calling for Christmas.

'How is your father after that business at the gallery? I knew he was going through an awful time after our last call and I did not want to irritate him by calling often.'

This attitude irked Viola the most, the presumption that reaching out to Placido was an irritation. It might have been to her, but her gracious father was unchanged in his warm regard for her mother.

'Papa would have loved to hear from you mother. It was a stressful time for him.'

'Where is he? May I speak to him now?'

'It's three in the morning, he's asleep. I will ask him to call you later.'

'I would prefer to call instead. We are going out to a New Year's Eve party in half an hour. You caught me as I was walking to the door. I will call your father once we have rested after our night out.'

Her high-flying mother was off to a start of the year party, and would have many more lined up in the months ahead. A quiet lifestyle that served Placido's creative life, never appealed to her.

Viola heard her stepfather call out to her mother to hurry.

They parted on good terms with Viola's acceptance that her mother would do things her way regardless of what she thought, or how she felt.

* * *

A week later, after the hype of the festive season had passed, Viola decided it was the right time to speak to Vanessa Smythe and Howard about her change of plans.

Vanessa Smythe's deepened frown, hardened by time, raised her eyes to Viola. In a startling, blood chilling lowered tone, she hissed.

'Ah, the business at Galleria Bardo makes you leave. Yes, I saw the news. Howard will sign you off.'

Her skeletal, disjointed movement to the door had Viola pondering, for the umpteenth time, on what had created this woman of stone.

She left the college that day with her sparse belongings, emotionless after her brief time in this organization.

Music was in her soul, her mission. She had to get back to teaching what fired her blood.

Matthew met Viola after her college meeting at the riverside. Madalena babysat Jungen for the day.

They walked to the laneway mural for Viola's last viewing of the street art that brought the past and present into sharp focus. Her empathy for Elio, the intriguing young market man in Mozambique led her into the world of his brother Eka.

Both gone in a violent blink.

Matthew respected her space to farewell the lives that moved her spirit in a way he did not understand.

He held her hand as they walked back to the bench at the riverside. She lay her head on his shoulder.

'Where to from here?'

She knew what he meant and sat with it for a while.

'What are you thinking? Talk to me.'

He looked away, out across the river, still holding her hand.

'Is there a place for *us* in your future?'

'I can't answer that just yet.'

'Can I at least hope?'

Viola knew if ever her heart was true, Matthew had the personality and sensitivity to be the person for her. But Australia was calling, and she had to heed the call.

'We can talk when I get back to Blackwater Ridge if that's okay with you.'

They said nothing more on that as they strolled back to Viola's apartment. She packed up her meagre belongings and headed back to the gallery.

Rob Dwyer's response to her confirmation that she will return to Blackwater by the beginning of the term solidified that this is what she had to do.

The days rolled on with the speed of many pleasant hours with her father, Matthew and Jungen. Placido invited him to stay at the gallery whenever he was in Porto.

Ariel took up the offer to work at the gallery with Placido while she ran her own business. She needed a place to call home, and he needed to have someone, someone he could trust and count on in this vast expanse of property he owned.

That her father would not be alone when she left, lightened her departure.

Matthew accepted that Viola was not ready to commit to anything but her work. She spent many nights wishing she could commit to a relationship.

Now was not the right time.

In her last poetry entry in her journal, before she left for Australia, she wrote a haiku conveying the depth and brevity of her relationships.

Heed the inner voice
when a call for help arrives
and so sweet love must wait...

The End

AFTERWORD

My passion for teaching and writing are closely aligned hence I thought I would share my perceptions on the role of teachers and why I created Viola Bardo as a teacher and justice seeker.

Teaching is never singular in the manifold duties as educator, nurturer, social justice initiator, carer, and person that a child/student/peer can trust. In my growing up years I have been blessed to have had teachers who opened my ears and eyes beyond the confines of a narrow-minded apartheid system. Equally my parents ensured that apartheid did not define the course of my life. It is as a consequence of my visionary mentors, the wonderful schools I attended, and the friendships forged that I uphold :

In our angst and joy we are ONE under the sky of humanity.

Within perceived or self-labeled imperfection lies a wealth of perfection. Teachers celebrate and grow this wealth in their students.

Fundamental to the role of a teacher is respect for all. This in turn generates self-respect and cradles students to exude the same.

All Lives Matter is drawn into my stories from this foundation of my teaching and childhood experiences in apartheid South Africa with an unstinting adherence to *Black Lives Matters,* regardless of where we live or work in the world.

Relationships are core to leadership and every teacher, every upholder of peace and justice, in any occupation, is a significant cog to a safe and secure society.

The fictional character, Viola Bardo, emulates the multifaceted duties of a teacher with music in her blood and justice in her soul in selflessly serving others.

SOULS OF HER DAUGHTERS
(TRILOGY OR STANDALONE NOVELS)

I f you enjoy trilogies, *Souls of Her Daughters Collection* may be read as a boxset ebook trilogy, or as standalone novels in print or ebook editions.

Souls of her Daughters:

A close bond between a mother and her daughters is shrouded in unforgotten terror, shame and secrets. Dr Grace Sharvin, and her social worker sister escape from South Africa to Australia but will they be free of the past when uninvited ghosts return to threaten their new lives?

Souls of her Daughters weaves the struggles of life in a poignant story of tears, fear, laughter and hope... a timeless tale of every woman's story — we are compassionate when we are vulnerable.

Chosen Lives is a novel that wrestles with hope for a New World Order amidst the fear of today. When an aircraft disappears, trust is compromised and tension escalates.

What Change May Come, *confronts the discomfort of irrepressible change, but time tells truths, begging for understanding.*

I f you've enjoyed reading, *Gallery Nights - (The Bardo Trilogy 2)* please leave an honest review to help other readers decide if they might like to read my books. This will help me to write more.

235

With Gratitude,

Mala Naidoo
 www.malanaidoo.com